JANE HETHERINGTON'S
ADVENTURES IN DETECTION: 3

A GAME OF
CAT AND MOUSE

NINA JON

ISBN: 0985120622
ISBN-13: 9780985120627

Contents

Chapter 1	Sisters! Sisters!	1
Chapter 2	Mad March Hare	5
Chapter 3	The Mouse in the Summerhouse	9
Chapter 4	Gone Fishing!	13
Chapter 5	A Game of Cat and Mouse	23
Chapter 6	Mousetrap	31
Chapter 7	The Case of the Sister Behaving Strangely	41
Chapter 8	Think Out of the Box	45
Chapter 9	Dabney Farm	49
Chapter 10	Lucy Erpingham	55
Chapter 11	Jill	63
Chapter 12	Stella Barnes	73
Chapter 13	The Bin Woman	77
Chapter 14	Tricky Mickey	81
Chapter 15	The Fig Leaf	89
Chapter 16	Hell's Angels?	93
Chapter 17	The Chase	101
Chapter 18	There's Only One Emma Greenlee	111
Chapter 19	Monty	115
Chapter 20	Patio-man	123
Chapter 21	Stan the Man	129
Chapter 22	The Mouse Catcher General!	139
Chapter 23	The Underwear Model	145

Chapter 24	Charlie Moon	149
Chapter 25	The Real McCoy	161
Chapter 26	Cauliflowers and Cabbages	175
Chapter 27	Mantrap	193
Chapter 28	Jane Sets her Trap	201
Chapter 29	The Bait is Taken	203
Chapter 30	Pete Lambert	207
Chapter 31	The Olive Branch	215
Chapter 32	Will No One Rid Me of this Turbulent Mouse?	219
Chapter 33	The Whine of the Mosquito	225
Chapter 34	That Old White Magick	229
Chapter 35	Saffron and Silk	241
Chapter 36	Mr Jonathan	245
Chapter 37	Month's End	251
Chapter 38	Shine On Charlie Moon!	255
Chapter 39	An Ode to the Artful Dodger	257

CHAPTER ONE

Sisters! Sisters!

I

In kitchen of her sister's house, eighteen-year-old Lucy Erpingham poured two glasses of white wine and carried them over to the table where her sister, Jodie Narbade, peeled cellophane away from a selection of dips.

"Jodie, would you say you're very much the older sister?" Lucy asked, slumping down in the chair next to Jodie.

"What makes you ask?" Jodie replied.

"Some new guy has started at work and I got talking to him and said you were six years older than me. He said with an age gap like that, he bet you'd always been very much the older sister – that's what he said – and I said, what you mean bossy?"

Jodie helped herself to a breadstick. She knew what her sister really wanted to talk about. "Do you like him – this new guy?"

"A bit."

"A bit, eh? How old is he?"

"Bit older than me."

"Has he got a girlfriend?"

1

Instead of replying, Lucy opened a bag of crisps, dunked one of them in some of the dip and popped it in her mouth.

"What's his name?" Jodie asked.

With a mouthful of food, Lucy mumbled something incomprehensible, to which Jodie raised her wineglass and said, "Here's to Lucy and Mmunamable!"

"Me and Mmunamable! I wish we could do this more often, Jodie. Get together like this."

"I'm always here for you Lucy, you know that, but I'm a married woman now, I'm not at your beck and call anymore, love."

"Yeah, but I need someone to confide in."

"Why? What have you done?" Jodie teased. "Is that the door?" she asked just as the front doorbell rang for the second time. "Who on earth can that be at this time?"

She answered the door to find her neighbour looking quite flustered.

"I'm so glad you're in Jodie," he said. "My battery's flat and I'm already late. I need somebody to jump it. Is your husband about?"

"No, he's at a stag night, but don't worry I've got leads in the back of my car. I'll just get my keys."

She picked up her keys from the hall table, and called out to her sister, "Lucy I'm just helping my neighbour jump-start his car. I won't be long."

"Okay," Lucy called back.

II

Less than fifteen minutes later, Jodie walked back into the kitchen with the words, "Got him started." Lucy wasn't there. "Lucy? Where are you?" she called out.

Nobody replied, and so she knocked on the door of the downstairs' cloakroom, but the door swung open, revealing an empty room. Lucy wasn't in the living room either. Jodie yelled upstairs: "Lucy? Are you up there?"

When she didn't hear anything, she ran up the stairs but her sister wasn't anywhere that she could see. She returned to the kitchen. It was a bit like the Marie Celeste – the wine bottle was where she'd left it, as were their snacks and wineglasses, both still two thirds full. Where on earth was she? She was about to say, "I think you're a bit old for hide and seek love," when she realised Lucy's handbag and coat were gone.

She called Lucy's mobile phone, but got the answer phone. "You gone home Lucy? Aren't you feeling very well?" she said. "At least call me and let me know you're okay." She sent the same message by text and received a reply by return.

'Had to go! Sorry. Things to do. C U!'

Jodie stared at the message. She'd never known her sister to do such a thing. It was completely out of character.

'What's happened? I'm here for you whatever you've done. But I can't help you if you won't tell me!' she immediately texted back.

She didn't get a reply and her calls went unanswered.

CHAPTER TWO

Mad March Hare

Jane Hetherington opened her bedroom curtains to see a hare sprinting across one of the fields adjoining the thatched cottage where she lived, and rabbits contentedly nibbling the newly emerged tips of the sugar beet crop. Farmer won't be pleased, she thought. The scene reminded her that it was the first day of March, and she must turn the pages of the various calendars she had around the house.

I wonder what the month will bring, she thought, once she'd made her way downstairs to sit in her kitchen and drink her first coffee of the morning. She opened the back door to allow the spring sunshine to flood in. She could hear the birds chirping in the garden outside, but other than this, the house was silent. When her husband Hugh was still alive, and her daughter Adele, still lived at home, the house had always been full of noise. Back in those days, she'd yearned for moments such as this one, but now she had it, she'd have swapped it in a thrice for an argument with her daughter over a phone bill, or the sound of her husband complaining that his glasses weren't where he'd left them and why couldn't anybody ever leave his things alone?

She picked up her coffee cup and walked over to the open door. Although only the beginning of the month, tulips had joined the bluebells in bringing colour to the winter garden. She glanced over to her summerhouse. Its slatted egg-shell blue walls were caught in the sun. She sipped her coffee, staring away in the distance. The hare and the rabbits had gone, and in their place a large dog fox glanced right and left, searching for breakfast. Was he in the farmer's pay, she wondered. She smiled to herself, closed her back door and took her coffee with her to her study.

Hopefully some new instructions would have arrived for her detective agency – the one she'd set up at sixty-three years of age – an age when many would be contemplating retirement. The agency had only been in existence for a couple of months, yet it had kept her busy enough, as was its purpose. To date she'd found missing people; revealed the person behind a string of poison-pen letters; unmasked a safe-breaker; caught a jewellery thief; established why lovers were distracted, and children unhappy at school. She'd even helped solve a murder. Nowadays this was all in a month's work for her.

She turned her computer on to find an e-mail from a Dean Moon, which immediately engrossed her.

'I'm writing to you about my seventy-nine-year-old grand-dad,' the e-mail began. 'It all started around about a month ago, when my granddad showed my mum a letter he'd got from his bank about the money he'd run up on his credit card. He admitted he'd had other letters from them, but he'd thrown them out 'cos he only keeps his credit card for emergencies. He thought because he didn't use it he could ignore the letters! He only showed mum the letter because the bank was

6

threatening to send the bailiffs round to his flat. Mum spoke to the bank manager. He said the card had been used by someone who'd run up massive debts. Granddad said it wasn't him. He hasn't got anything to spend that much money on and there's certainly nothing to show for it. He thinks someone must have been going into his flat and helping themselves to the card and putting it back. Even though we all told him not to, he keeps the card in a drawer in the lounge. It was still there when he looked. The staff all have keys – it might have been one of them, or some keys might have been left lying around by someone. Also, Granddad's getting pretty absent-minded. He's taken to leaving a key under a flowerpot in a neighbour's garden! For all we know, he may even have gone out one day and left the front door unlocked. Turns out, the same thing's happened to other people there. Granddad's certain it must be someone where he lives, who was watching his comings and goings. That does seem the most likely – the cards were used and put back more than once – but it could have been a gang who've moved on. We called the police and they interviewed all the staff, but no one's been charged. The police say their investigations are continuing, but I'm not sure they're treating it as urgently as I think they should. I think they're waiting to see if the thief strikes again before they expend valuable manpower on it. The complex's on alert, so if the thief is still around, he or she has gone to ground for the moment.

The bank and credit card company have written-off Granddad's debt, but they've cancelled his cards. I've never seen Granddad so angry. "Someone steals from me and I get the blame!" he said. That's why I'm writing to you. I want you to find out if Granddad's right, and it was someone he knows.

There's more to this than I care to put in an e-mail. Mum's taken Granddad away for a couple of weeks to cheer him up. Can we meet up when he gets back? Since Nan died a couple of years ago, Granddad's lived in sheltered accommodation. Can we meet there?'

Not only did Jane believe she should help a vulnerable old man if she could, but the case sounded intriguing, particularly the words – There's more to this than I care to put in an e-mail. She accepted the case immediately.

CHAPTER THREE

The Mouse in the Summerhouse

Jane decided to throw open her summerhouse door to let the spring air into it. She unlocked the door for the first time since October, and came face to face with a mouse busy scuttling across the floor. Both mouse and woman froze. Once she'd have jumped on a chair and called out to her husband, but since his death, she had to deal with situations such as this herself. In any event, sciatica made it impossible for her to lumber up on to a chair nowadays, let alone jump. She looked around the room and saw an empty plastic flowerpot discarded nearby. It was within reach. She picked it up and knelt down in front of the mouse.

"Come little friend," she said in a whisper. "Let's release you into the wild."

When the mouse made no attempt to move, she tried to drop the flowerpot over it, but missed. The mouse immediately scuttled behind a heavy book case, which took up most of one wall. No amount of coaxing from Jane would budge him and the case was too heavy for her to move single-handedly. Of course she could leave the door open and wait for the mouse to leave, but she was looking for an excuse to pay her next door neighbour Charity, a visit, and now she had one.

Charity Parsons was a hairdresser in her early twenties. With both her parents dead, Charity was raising her school-boy brother, Jack, single-handedly. Charity had a boyfriend called Johnny Lambert. Johnny was good looking and charming and Jane had always got on very well with him. Nothing was too much trouble for him and he could be kind beyond compare. But where Jane was unable to defend Johnny was in his treatment of Charity and Jack. This was shabby. In her view, there was no other word for it. He'd left Charity more than once – the last time being a couple of months earlier, when he'd summarily announced that he'd bought himself a one-way ticket to the Falkland Islands, because he wanted to see 'more of the world'. Jane put this fecklessness down to his dislocated childhood than to any wander lust, but it left Charity and Jack heartbroken. Charity had sworn she wouldn't take him back again no matter what, and Jane thought the relationship finally over. But Johnny was back, wanting to reconcile and twenty-four hours after turning up unannounced at Charity's door, his motorbike was still parked outside Charity's cottage.

Jane pushed open the gate at the rear of Charity's cottage garden, and walked up the garden path to her backdoor.

"Jane!" Charity said, when she found her neighbour on her back door step.

"As I understand Johnny is back, I wonder if I may have a word with him," Jane said as innocently as she could. "I have an unwanted intruder in my house..."

When Charity looked alarmed, Jane added, "...he's about so long," she motioned with her fingers, "and has a tail as long as he is. I've named him Aleckski because he's the mouse who came in from the cold. I wondered if Johnny might help me remove him – dealing with wild animals is man's work, after all."

"Johnny's not here. Jack's school's closed for teacher training, and Johnny's taken him fishing. But come in, come in."

No sooner had Jane stepped through the door, than Charity said, "Now before you say anything, I want to get one thing out of the way. I know what I said, but I love Johnny, and he must love me, otherwise he wouldn't keep coming back. He told Jack he missed us when he was in the Falklands and that's why he came back. He came back to be with us. He's not as young as he used to be. He thinks it's time he settled down, and it's me he wants to settle down with. They were his very words."

"Well I'm certainly glad to hear that. You know I want nothing more than to see you happily settled down, Charity," Jane said.

"Let's not get too carried away. We'll just take it slowly for the time being. I don't want him thinking he can just pick up where he left off, every time he wants to. We'll see..." Charity said, suddenly preoccupied with her own thoughts. "He does get on so well with Jack, and he has other skills as well..." she added, with a backwards kick of her leg and a giggle, her usual gaiety having returned.

"Try and remember I'm a respectable widow woman, young lady," Jane replied, as sternly as she could manage.

CHAPTER FOUR

Gone Fishing!

"Lucky we're wearing waterproof boots," Jack said, as he and Johnny trudged across a water-laden field towards the river they'd selected for their fishing trip. It had rained heavily overnight, and the ground was quite damp underfoot.

As Jack spoke, he took a step forward and the ground beneath his right foot sank rapidly. He'd stepped into a puddle much deeper than he'd realised, and when he tried to pull his right foot out, he couldn't – it was stuck. The water was rising alarmingly. It had almost reached the top of his wellington boots. "I'm stuck!" he yelled, almost overbalancing. He would have fallen head first into the water had Johnny not grabbed him by his collar.

Still holding onto Jack's collar, Johnny took a hold of Jack's wellington boot and pulled it out of the puddle. Jack took a couple of steps backwards to regain his balance. "Now that was lucky!" he said.

The two carried on. When they reached the river bank, they threw a tarpaulin over the only dry piece of ground they could find and set up their fishing equipment as best they could. Each unfolded stools. The cold box containing both bait and lunch was placed next to Johnny's chair, and it was he who baited both his and Jack's rod. Minutes later the two were sitting next to each other, surrounded by fishing paraphernalia, lines cast in the water, their rods resting on the rod perch planted between the two stools. Neither spoke.

After a while Johnny ruffled Jack's hair and said, "You realise that you and me are effectively brothers-in-law."

"Don't do that," Jack said, smoothing down his hair with his hands. "Do brothers-in-law give each other advice on girls?" Jack asked, a few moments later.

Johnny broke into a grin. No wonder Jack was suddenly so self-conscious of his appearance. His girlfriend's little brother was in love. Bless, he thought. But then Jack was nearly fourteen, he remembered.

"What's her name?" Johnny asked.

"Polly. She's in my class. She's very pretty and she makes me laugh," he said, shyly.

"She the most popular girl in school?" Johnny asked.

"Not really, but I like her."

"She the girl you texted me about?"

Jack nodded.

"She know you like her?"

Jack shook his head.

"Why don't you tell her?"

"She might like someone else more," Jack mumbled.

"Well that my friend is what we call life," Johnny said, leaning back in his seat, pleased with his rapport with Jack, who he thought of as a mate. He was rather taken aback then by Jack's response to this comment, which Jack clearly found glib.

"That it?" Jack said furiously. He stood up. "That your great advice is it? Ask her out and if she says no, tough. Get over it!"

"Jack, no mate, that's not what I meant," Johnny said. He hadn't realised how much Jack liked this girl. He jumped to his feet, tripped over his stool and fell over. "I just meant, well…" he tried to say, still sprawled on the muddy ground.

"I should have known better than to turn to you for relationship advice," Jack snapped, turning on his heels and walking away, splashing angrily through the puddles.

"Where are you going?" Johnny yelled after him. "We're in the middle of nowhere!"

"I'm going for a slash," Jack yelled back. "You going to still be here when I get back or will you have gone to South America again on a whim?"

Jack's anger stunned Johnny, and his comments wounded him. They were a bit too close for comfort. He flinched. He stood up, brushed himself down and righted his stool. He sat down to kick the ground in shame. Jack was just a kid, and a kid who'd been through a hell of a lot. He'd lost his dad when still a youngster, and his mum not much later. Charity had effectively given up her girlhood to raise him. She'd shown the type of maturity that Johnny finally realised was lacking in himself. Charity had done a fantastic job bringing up Jack. The fact that she'd been prepared to do this said everything about her. It hadn't been easy for either of them, and Johnny's immaturity couldn't have helped matters. This he now understood. It had taken a trip to South America to make him understand that what he saw as an irreverent, devil-may-care, take on life, was no more than self-obsession and selfishness, but realise it he finally did. The idea behind the fishing trip had been to tell Jack this, but now Jack wasn't speaking to him.

When Jack returned he ignored Johnny. He didn't even make eye contact. He clattered into his seat and reeled his line in, angrily tossing the hook and line into the air behind him and flipping it back into the water. A stony silence descended.

"I was out of order mate," Johnny said. "I didn't take you seriously. I'm sorry."

"You don't take life seriously, that's your problem, Johnny."

"Point taken," Johnny said. By way of a peace offering, Johnny offered him a sandwich. "Peanut butter and sausage. Your favourite."

Jack snatched a sandwich from him and bit into it. He was still fuming as he finished off the last mouthful, almost swallowing it whole. Johnny poured a mug of steaming soup out for him. Jack scowled at him, but took it from Johnny and sipped it.

"Okay," Johnny said. "My advice sucked. Let's start again. Have you told her you like her?"

Jack shook his head. "I've already told you, I haven't," he said crossly.

"Does she have a boyfriend?"

Jack shook his head.

"Good. What does she like doing? Hobbies and stuff."

"Same stuff I do."

"So she likes football and girls then?" Johnny teased him.

"No," Jack said, mellowing. "I meant music and stuff. She seems to spend a lot of time surrounded by other girls. Boy, girls can talk."

"They sure can. And not just girls, so can adult women, mate, believe me."

"What do they talk about?" Jack wanted to know.

"Boys mostly, so I'm led to believe. She a member of any clubs that you know of or the like?"

"She spends quite a lot of time in coffee places with her friends, or social networking, but I haven't picked up the nerve to ask to be her friend yet."

"Right," Johnny said. "We know a couple of things about her. She likes coffee and company."

"And she hasn't got a boyfriend," Jack reminded him.

"And she hasn't got a boyfriend," Johnny repeated. "Okay," he said, putting his arm around Jack's shoulder in a fatherly manner. "You need to approach her when she's alone, at the lockers or something. Ask her if she wants to have a coffee with you."

"What if she says no?"

"We'll cross that bridge if we come to it. I had to ask your sister out more than once before she said yes, remember. Ask her if she would like to have a coffee with you sometime. Now this is important. When she says yes, and I'm sure she will," he added quickly, before Jack had a chance to say anything further. "When she says yes, or more likely – sure, why not! – which is the kind of things girls say so they don't seem too keen, you need to have somewhere in mind. Where does she normally go?"

"The place on the high street, above the bookshop."

"Right, well don't take her there then, otherwise you'll end up having a date with all her friends as well as her. Take her somewhere she doesn't normally go. Doesn't have to be in Failsham. Tell her you'll either pick her up from her house or meet her there, whatever she'd prefer. Be early. When she turns up, tell her she looks really nice – whether she does or not. Pay for her coffee and remember to ask her about herself. Doesn't matter if you already know, ask her anyway. Ask her what she likes to do, what she wants to do when she leaves school, who her favourite bands and TV shows are, etc. Even ask her if she likes cats, that kind of thing. Only talk about yourself if she asks and then be honest and modest. Girls hate show-offs. Does that help?" he said, his hand resting on Jack's head.

"You're okay, Johnny, even though you're an ugly bugger. I'm sorry I yelled at you," he said playfully punching him.

"It's okay, mate – I guess I deserved it. Well, as you've confided in me, I'm going to tell you what happened when I was in the Falkland Islands, which changed me. Do you think I've changed?" Johnny asked. When Jack didn't reply immediately, Johnny said, "Well I have."

Jack looked over at Johnny. He was wondering what on earth he was going to say and hoping it was something he actually wanted to hear. For his part, Johnny had jumped off his stool to lie stretched over the tarpaulin by the side of river bank, staring up at the sky above, blinking rapidly in the sunlight. For a few moments, all Jack could hear was the rushing of the stream, and the birds chirping overhead.

"Are you sitting comfortably?" Johnny asked.

Jack, perched on his canvas stool, nodded and grinned.

"Then I'll begin," Johnny said, adjusting the waterproof cap he always wore to go fishing. "When I was in the Falklands, I ended up staying at some commune run by some Christian

Fellowship. I hadn't realised this when I booked it. I wondered why it was so cheap."

Jack giggled.

"Yeah, well anyway," Johnny continued. "One of the things about the commune was that we used to eat together in a communal dining room at long tables, like at boarding school. One evening, I had dinner opposite a young American couple. Her name was Tami and his was Billy. They were Born-Again Christians or something. Despite both only being about thirty, they already had four kids and another on the way. I'd just sat down to eat, when Billy asked me if I was married and had any kids. I said no. I mentioned I'd had a girlfriend, but we'd split up 'cos I couldn't offer her the commitment she wanted, with me not being the marrying type, a rolling stone who gathers no moss, and that kind of rubbish. I laughed at my words, but no one else did. Then, mate, suddenly out of the blue, Billy asked me whether I liked my father, like there was some connection between that and what I'd just said. The question caught me off-guard. 'Don't know him,' I said, which is the truth, as you know. I told them how he'd walked out when I was a little kid and I hadn't seen him since, and didn't even know if he was dead or alive. I said I'd seen some photographs of him, and I looked a bit like him and stuff, but that was all I knew. At this point, I realised that everyone at the table was listening and looking at me expectantly. Billy basically repeated the same question. 'But do you like your father? The man you know him to be?' he said. 'The man who basically abandoned me and my mum?' I asked. 'Yes,' he said. 'That man. Do you like him?'

"I was honest, mate," Johnny said to Jack. "I said that I didn't like him, no. In fact, I hated him for what he did to me and mum. Now this is where it gets weird, man," Johnny said, pointing his finger at Jack. "Billy looked me straight in the eyes, he had these piercing blue eyes, mate, I tell you. He said, 'If you don't like your father, why are you allowing yourself to turn into him?'

"I didn't know what to say. You know me mate. I always have something to say, but not this time Jack. Speechless I was, speechless. Eventually I recovered and spluttered, 'But I'm not like him. Am I? I haven't abandoned my missus and kid,' trying to justify the way I was. At this stage, the whole table was staring at me calmly, quizzically like. The whole place had gone quiet. It was surreal. Billy carried on talking. 'My dad was a drunken wastrel,' he said. 'He'd disappear for weeks on end at a time. One day he didn't come back at all. He eventually reappeared one night, months later, asking me to go with him, but I wouldn't leave Mom. From that day on, I could count on my fingers the times I saw him. He didn't pay a penny in maintenance, and no amount of Court Orders would make him. On the few occasions he arranged to see us, he rarely turned up and when he did it was only to ask my mother for money, usually to pay off his debts. It broke her heart and my sisters' hearts. It was harder on them than me. They really hoped he'd come back into their lives and be the dad they'd always wanted, and he kept promising them he would. But he didn't. By the time I was thirteen, I vehemently disliked my father. I have made sure, from that day to this, that I don't behave the way my dad did. I've absolutely no desire to allow myself to turn into that man.'

"I didn't know what to say, Jack. I tried to steer the conversation away from me. 'Is your dad still alive?' I asked Billy. He and Tami shook their heads. 'He died a few years back,' Billy said. 'I visited him in hospital before he passed over. I didn't want to, but my very sensible wife said I should make my peace with him and I'm glad I did. But I'll tell you something else, Jonathan. I'm gladder still that I fought all my life against being him. My life is better for it' he said, taking his wife's hand in his and kissing it. I thought he'd finished with me, but he hadn't. He continued to stare at me, not judgementally you understand, more expectantly like. Everyone at the table was all weirdly calm, like I said. 'I must ask you again, Jonathan, why are you allowing yourself to turn into him, a man you clearly dislike?' Billy asked. 'But I'm not,' I said, indignantly. 'Aren't you?' Billy said. 'You entered into a relationship with a young woman, allowing her to believe the relationship had a future, caused her to fall in love with you, and allowed her young brother to look upon you as a father. Yet here you are, with them no longer a part of your life, which was your choice, not theirs.'

"I tell you man, I was sweating. 'If you put it like that,' I said, real subdued like. 'I didn't know I was becoming like him, but I can sort of see where you're coming from.' Billy left it at that. I'm not a self-conscious person, Jack, as you know, but man, I'm sure I was bright red by the end of it."

"That why you came back?" Jack asked, referring to Johnny's unexpectedly return from the South Atlantic. Johnny sat up.

"It was, mate. It was. I did a lot of thinking that night and pretty much every night since. I realised Billy was right. I was turning into my father, a man I hate. I don't want that to happen. I don't want to end up like him and I do want you and

21

your sister in my life. So, I promise you that for as long as it's in my power to do so, I will be there for you and your sister for the rest of my life, as long as you want me in it, of course."

Jack gazed at Johnny. He was bathed in sunlight. At that moment, Jack couldn't have thought more of him, if Johnny had been his own father. Johnny jumped up abruptly. Something was tugging on Jack's line.

"I don't believe it," he said, reaching out to hold onto Jack's fishing rod. "You've got a bite, lad!"

Jack stood up to steady the line. With Johnny behind him, he pulled in a small pink trout. Jack quickly unhooked the small wriggling fish and held it in his hands. With the fish still thrashing in Jack's hands, and Jack grinning, Johnny captured the moment on camera.

"Best chuck that back in, mate," he said.

Jack did. "I'm sure Jane could help you find your father, if you wanted to find him," he said.

"Why would I want to do that?" Johnny asked, surprised that Jack had even suggested it.

"To make your peace with him, like Billy did. You never know, he might be sick. Look what happened to my mum. Anyway, if you want to, ask Jane. She's very good at that kind of thing. She'd probably give you a cut-price deal," he added, grinning.

CHAPTER FIVE

A Game of Cat and Mouse

I

A few hours after Jane paid Charity a visit, Charity visited Jane with both Johnny and Jack in tow. Jack clutched a fishing net. Jane joined them in her back garden.

"Understand you've got a mouse problem, Jane," Johnny said, as though he'd just returned from a weekend away rather than South America.

"It's good to see you back, Johnny," Jane said. "He's in the summerhouse, behind a bookshelf unless he's moved. I want to make sure there isn't a colony nesting behind there, but I am going to need some help moving the shelves. Would you mind? I've cleared the books out already."

The party made its way to the summerhouse, where after some discussion, they took their positions. Charity held a plastic box, and Jack his net. They stood to the right and the left of the bookshelf, while Jane waited by the open back door, broom in hand, to help the mouse on his or her way outside.

Johnny put one hand on the sturdy bookshelf, and the other behind it. The bookshelf was easily as tall as six-foot Johnny, and even with his arms outstretched, as wide.

"This thing's heavy so I am going to have to edge it forward, one side at a time. He's likely to scarper soon as I move the bookshelf, so you'll need to be ready," Johnny said.

Jack and Charity made ready to catch the tiny animal when it ran out from its hiding place. Both squatted, their attention entirely focused on the bookshelf. Jack raised his net above his head and Charity lowered the box, ready to slam dunk any rodent which appeared.

"On the count of three. Three!" Johnny yelled, moving the bookshelf an inch forward. "Ready, he'll run out any second, now," warned Johnny, as the bookshelf crept forward another inch.

Jack and Charity leaned forward, as though skiers about to slalom. Both tightened their grips on net and box respectively. Jane gripped on to her broom handle as the bookshelf edged forward, the tension mounting as bit by bit the bookshelf edged away from the wall. But nothing happened.

Jack asked, "Where is it?"

"It's hiding, mate," Johnny said. "It's probably terrified. One more shove and I'll be able to check behind it. Be careful – he, or they, may suddenly dart out."

Johnny moved the bookshelf until he could peer behind it. But there was no sign of a mouse or a nest.

"Anything?" Charity asked.

"Nothing," he said. "Let's pull it right out to make sure."

Johnny dragged the bookshelf into the middle of the floor and everyone gathered to stare at the space created. A few droppings were all there were to show a mouse had ever been there. There certainly wasn't any sign of a nest.

"I'm so sorry," Jane said. "I've got you all over here on a wild goose chase, or rather a wild mouse chase."

"Don't think anything of it. Help me push the shelf back, will you, Jack?" Johnny said.

"Best we have a double-check before we leave, in case there's a colony hiding somewhere," Charity said.

The other furniture in the summerhouse consisted of three comfy chairs, a corner cabinet and a coffee table. They moved each piece of furniture, and checked for mice. Johnny even stood on a chair to check the inside of lampshade. After the extensive search ended with no sign of a mouse or a nest, all agreed it had been a solitary mouse who had moved on.

"If he reappears we'll come back and get him," Johnny said.

"Yeah, like the flying squad," Jack said. "Can I go now?"

"Yeah, you push off, Jack," Charity said. "Johnny and I want to talk to Jane about something anyway."

II

With Jack gone, the others moved to Jane's kitchen.

"Johnny was thinking about tracing his father. To make his peace with him. Do you think he could find him after all this time?" Charity asked, glancing at Johnny.

Unusually for him, he was silent. His hands were stretched out on Jane's kitchen table and his head bowed.

"It might be possible, even after all this time. It goes without saying that I'll do everything I can to help."

25

A short silence ensued, broken by Charity saying, "Thing is, Johnny doesn't know if he wants to or not."

"If that son-of-a-bitch didn't give a damn about what happened to us, why should I care what happened to him?"

Charity and Jane glanced at each other.

"Really you shouldn't," Charity said. "But if you want to get things sorted out in your mind, you might have to. He's still your dad. It's natural..." She stopped talking.

Jane wasn't sure how she'd feel if she was in Johnny's situation. She knew Charity had only once approached her boyfriend on the subject of his father, to which the mumbled reply had been: 'I'd like to know why he went, but I might end up hating him even more if I knew, so it's probably best I don't.' Charity had never mentioned the subject again.

Jane studied Johnny. She understood his indecision. Johnny's father had abandoned his family when Johnny was just out of nappies, and had made no attempt to contact them. Rationally, he should not want to have anything to do with his father, but he was a human being, and human emotions were more powerful than mere rationality. Wasn't it only psychopaths who were entirely rational, she reflected. Johnny wasn't a psychopath, and it was perfectly understandable that he'd want to meet his father, if only to see his face and hear his voice, yet equally understandable that he should be reluctant to do so, after what his father had done to him.

"It was Jack who put the idea into my head," Johnny said. "And now the idea is there, I can't get it out."

"You don't need to explain," Jane said. "Of course you still think about him, wondering where he is and the type of person he is. He won't be the same person he was back then, you realise?"

"Bleeding hope not," Johnny said.

"I'll support you whatever you do," Charity said.

"So you said," Johnny mumbled.

Jane attended to the coffee. It had stood for long enough. She poured three cups, adding some milk to Charity and Johnny's coffee, and serving hers black. "I do believe I have some garibaldi biscuits somewhere," she said, getting up to open one of the kitchen cupboards. "If you want, I could try and find out if your father is still alive, and where he is." Charity shot a glance in Jane's direction. "If I manage to find something, then you can decide whether or not to get in touch. Here they are," she said, referring to the biscuits. "Let me get some plates."

Jane rejoined them at the table, a biscuit tin in one hand, and three side plates in the other.

"My dad's name is Peter Mark Lambert, although he was always known as Pete. I haven't seen him since I was two," Johnny said. "He was a lot older than my mum. If he's still alive he'd be sixty."

"These are the only photographs Johnny has of his dad," Charity said, pushing an envelope over to Jane. She opened it. The envelope contained a couple of photographs: one of Johnny's parents' marriage, and the other of a young smiling couple with their new baby cradled in his mother's arms.

"That's me. Beautiful baby wasn't I?" he joked.

"Is your mother still alive?" Jane asked, ashamed that she didn't know. Johnny shook his head sadly.

"Died a few years back. It was ..." his sentence ended with him pretending to knock back an imaginary drink, indicating that his poor mother had been an alcoholic, who had drunk herself to death.

"I'm sorry," Jane said. "Does your father have any relatives that you know of?"

"He has a half-sister, Stella. She's a lot younger than him, but as far as I know she's not heard from him since the day he left Mum. We still exchange birthday cards and Christmas cards, so I'd know if he'd made contact with her. Except for one postcard, no-one's heard from him since the day he left."

"Postcard?" Jane asked.

"Yeah, get this," Charity interrupted. "His mum received a postcard from Blackpool a year after he left. What a ..." she said, her sentence trailing out, realising that her view on the subject was best left unsaid.

"What did the card say?" Jane asked.

"Hello from Blackpool! Nothing else," Johnny said. "He didn't even bother signing it. He just sent it to her as though to say, in case you were wondering, I'm still alive and enjoying life."

Now it was Charity's time to bow her head.

"How thoughtless and cruel," Jane said.

"That's my father."

Jane asked if he still had the card. Charity took the envelope from her and shook it until a postcard fell out. The picture on the card was a photograph of Johnny's father as a younger man, with his face pushed through a hardboard image of the cartoon cat *Tom,* pretending to chase *Jerry,* played by an unknown woman. Jane turned card over. The shot had been taken at a funfair in Blackpool.

"If your father is still alive and living under his own name, it will be quite easy to find him. We can search against his name, and see what comes up. I subscribe to a database of everyone in the UK telephone book and on the unedited electoral register. I can also find out if he's remarried, or unfortunately died. However, if he's living overseas, or under an assumed name, or he's one of those itinerant people who don't have a bank account or a fixed abode, then it's going to be much harder to find him, even impossible, unless we get some luck. I can start straight away if you want me to."

Johnny looked as though he was still undecided.

"I think you at least need to know if he's still alive, love," Charity said. "You can't decide what to do until we at least know that."

"Well, look who's here," Jane said, referring to Addison, Charity's jet black cat, who had just presented itself at her glass back door. The cat patted the door once with its paw, to let it be known that he wanted to be let in.

"Addison! Mate!" Johnny said, letting him in. The cat meowed once and ran into the kitchen. Charity patted her lap, but the cat surveyed all those in the kitchen only to ignore them and run over to the door which led into the utility room. Jane opened it for him with the words, "If the mouse is still around, hopefully Addison will see him off."

"Polish him off, more like," Charity said.

The cat ran into the utility room and jumped straight up onto the top of Jane's boiler and settled himself down on the cushion left for him there.

"All right for some," all three said simultaneously.

III

Her neighbours departed (leaving their sleeping cat behind). Two new cases in one day, thought Jane, not that Johnny's plight could be considered a case – that was more a matter of helping out an old friend.

She decided to start with a search against the name Pete(r) Mark Lambert. There were a number of entries. She opened and read some. The majority related to a famous US Country and Western singer, too young to be Johnny's father. She then carried out a search against his name on her UK database, which was as inclusive as anything could be. It revealed numerous names, any one of which could have been Johnny's father. Even after categorising them by age, there was nothing to differentiate one from the other. If she were going to knock on the door of every address listed, she'd end up crisscrossing the entire country and probably end up with many an earful or worse. This was not going to be easy, she realised.

She sent Charity a text message. 'Do you have any more information about Johnny's father, which might help me narrow down the search?' Charity replied: 'Only that his father was born in Hemsley, and worked as a docker there, before moving up here and marrying J's ma.'

This was something to go on at least. Jane glanced at her watch. Good heavens. It was much later than she'd thought. She'd suspend her search for the day and resume it in the morning.

She turned her computer off, drew her curtains and closed the study door behind her.

CHAPTER SIX

Mousetrap!

I

The next morning, Jane visited her summerhouse to ensure the mouse really had left it. A quick glance inside told her the answer, and she was soon in the small front room of her neighbour's house.

"To ensure the mouse really had gone, I left half a digestive biscuit on the summerhouse floor last night," she explained, "and this morning all that was left were some crumbs and a pile of mouse droppings. I can't just leave it – it'll breed, if it hasn't already. I'll be overrun."

"You did close the window, didn't you?" Johnny asked her. "They home you know."

"Of course. I checked they were closed, before I locked the door."

"I always check the windows last thing," Charity said. "Sometimes I have to get up in the night to double-check they're closed. When Johnny wasn't here I spent more time padding around the house checking the window locks were on, than I did asleep."

Johnny ignored her. He picked up a copy of British Mammals from the book shelf.

"First know your enemy," he said, flicking through the book. "Could it have been a pine martin?" he joked, studying the relevant page.

"Not unless we're in Scotland," Jane replied.

"No chance that it was actually a rat?"

"None, unless it's a pygmy rat."

"Is this your foe?" Johnny asked, holding out a page for her to study. She put her glasses on. The animal depicted was a tiny rodent with a short golden body, round ears and short legs, described as a harvest mouse. Its underbelly was white and its eyes bead-like and black. The entry went on to state that its numbers had declined sharply and that such rodents were no longer as common as they once were, and were now limited to isolated parts of the country.

"That's him!" Jane said.

"A single litter can contain up to ten youngsters," Johnny read out. "Let's hope he doesn't get himself a girlfriend."

"Or isn't already pregnant," Jane said, with a shudder.

"I can go and buy a mouse trap right now, if you want, or some poison."

"That's cruel!" squealed Charity, adding quickly, "although I entirely understand, if you choose to go down that route, Jane."

"Charity's right. It's too cruel," Jane said. "I know it's irrational, but I've looked into his or her little face. I almost feel I know him. The book says they're declining in numbers. There must be a more humane way to deal with this than kill him."

"I will cogitate, my dear," Johnny said

II

Jane left her neighbours investigating humane mouse removal, and returned home to continue her search for Johnny's father. She typed *UK Docks* into her search engine. This brought up numerous entries, including a detailed description about how to dock a dog's tail (which she chose not to read), and another on how to kill dock weeds and stop them from returning (which she printed off to put with her gardening books). She was unconcerned with the history of naval dockyards, the travelogue of a cargo container, nor with spacecrafts docking, nor the *Olympic Mentor* coming into dock. None of these would progress her search. She opened a webpage said to list every trading dock in Britain past and present. From it she accessed a page dedicated to the Newcastle Docks, and studied the names and photographs of its staff. All were far too young to be Johnny's father.

From there, Jane visited the websites of each of the docks in the UK. Even though Johnny's father would now be sixty, and was unlikely to still be employed in any of them, she thought it worth a chance. However, after hours in front of her computer, she was no further forward in her search. She searched *Dockworkers.* This produced images of dock workers across the world, information about various charities and a link to the blog of a dock worker, dedicated to the memory of his great grandfather, also a dock worker. Whilst many of the entries were fascinating, none of them helped her. There was nothing in any of these pages which drew her closer to Johnny's father. She searched under 'Stevedore' and learned nothing more than how to tie a stevedore knot. She even typed 'Longshoremen' but again drew a blank.

She was quite relieved to be interrupted by someone ringing her front door. She answered the door to a local resident called Hayley Paine. Hayley was in her early twenties, and had until recently, worked in a local supermarket until she was abruptly fired. There'd been rumours of money missing from a till, but nothing official. No charges were brought, and the young woman herself would tell all who listened that she was the victim of persecution, a smear campaign. Jane wondered what Hayley could want from her. Nothing positive, she suspected. "Hello. It's Hayley isn't it?" she asked.

"You're a private detective now, aren't you?" Hayley replied. Although a question, the words were spoken in such a direct manner that they came across almost as an accusation.

"An amateur private detective, yes."

"Yeah, well that's why I'm here. A proper one would be too expensive, wouldn't they?" Hayley replied.

Whilst Jane would rather not have been having this conversation, she was too polite to brush the girl aside. "How can I help you?" she asked.

"I want you to get some dirt on my cousin," Hayley said, pulling out a photograph of her cousin, which she held out to Jane. "Miss Goody two shoes. The family's golden girl. Miss can't put a foot wrong. Miss 'I'm engaged to the wonderful Adam, and we're going to go into business together. Isn't my life wonderful?'"

Jane looked at the photograph of Hayley's cousin: Jess Payne. A very pretty girl, Jane had always thought. She hadn't heard she was engaged. She must send a card, she thought, almost oblivious to Hayley's tirade, which was continuing unabated: "Lucky Adam, that's what I say. Lucky Adam! Lucky Adam!" she repeated, in a contemptuous and sneering tone.

Jane stared at the girl. How young she was to be so consumed by such petty jealousies. "What do you want me to do, Hayley?" she asked.

"Find something that will split them up. Something I can use to wipe that smug look off her face!"

Jane doubted if there were any skeletons worth knowing about in Jess Payne's cupboard, besides which, she had no intention of becoming involved in anything so underhand, and frankly, so silly.

"I'm terribly sorry, my dear, but I don't think I'm going to be able to take your case on," she said briskly. "I'm really rather busy at the moment. But thank you for thinking about me."

Hayley glared at her, and opened her mouth to reply, but wasn't given the opportunity. Jane firmly shut the door on her, hoping that would be the end of things, but wondering if it would.

She returned to her study and resumed her search by typing *Dockworkers* again. Jane's own grandfather had been a docker until his early death had plunged his widow and children into penury. She opened and read an entry about life on the docks from that era. It was fascinating. She could have spent hours reading it, but although it managed to be both poignant and funny in places, reading it was distracting her from her search, which was going nowhere fast.

She studied the postcard of Johnny's father again. Something told her it held a clue as to his whereabouts, but she couldn't think what.

35

Someone was knocking at her back door. She went to answer it, hoping she wasn't going to find Hayley Payne there. She didn't. Instead she found Johnny and Jack.

Jack was holding a tray over which a cloth was covering up a very strangely shaped object. Even more bizarrely, Johnny was holding the children's box game *Mousetrap*, on top of which was a wastepaper bin. Jane invited them in, feeling it best she let them speak first. Johnny placed the game on the table, the bin beside it, and next to that Jack's tray.

"I couldn't find a shop selling humane traps in Failsham, so I dug out an old game of *Mousetrap!* Instead," he explained.

"I'm not sure that was designed to trap real mice, Johnny," Jane pointed out, rather obviously, she thought once she'd said it.

"Oh ye of little faith," he replied. "I should tell you that my able assistant and I have been able to create a number of traps from this humble game, each more than capable of catching a real mouse. My able assistant will now produce our first trap. We'll start with the toy box, boy," he instructed.

Jack produced a bright yellow plastic box, which was about the size of three match boxes stacked on top of each other, and secured together by elastic bands, with a hinged door which opened at the top. Johnny took over.

"We figured two plastic mice must be about the size of one real one," Johnny said, picking up a couple of the game's tiny plastic rodent contestants to show her. The mice, both bi-peds, wore hard hats and boxing gloves. "Please note the front door is hinged, so if I do this" … he flicked the door and let it go… "you will see how it snaps straight back into place."

He flicked the door open a number of times, and each time it immediately snapped shut again. Jane opened her mouth to speak, only to be silenced by Johnny.

"One minute please. If we set it at an angle…" He set the door at a forty-five degree angle "… mousey can get in for his dinner, but he can't get out again. Watch and see – I mean watch and admire!"

He pushed two plastic mice into the toy box in quick succession. When the second mouse hit the back of the box, the door snapped closed.

"See!" Jack said gleefully.

"If that was a real mouse, he couldn't get out again unless he was bright enough to work out that if he climbs up the door, he can push it open from the top, which is unlikely in something with a brain the size of a pea, but just in case he is a rodent genius, we have two more, yes I said two more traps," Johnny roared in a mock evil laugh.

Jane said nothing.

The first of the other traps was produced. Jane picked it up and looked at it. It was a tiny plastic toilet sat atop a plastic cistern, with another high-walled rectangular box below, around which Johnny had thickly wrapped duct tape. A hole in the toilet basin, wide enough for a ball bearing, was the contraption's only entrance and exit. "It's a small hole but a mouse can make himself smaller. They can make themselves small enough to climb in and out of keyholes," he explained.

Jane had heard this, although in all her years of country living she had never yet come across a mouse squeezing itself through a keyhole and thought it unlikely she ever would.

"I've named it the Inescapable Box. We'll put grain at the bottom to tempt him in. Once in, he'll never be able to climb back out again – it's too slippery."

"Are you sure this box is really inescapable?"

"Not entirely."

"Show her the piece de resistance," Jack said, adding, "He's been working on this all afternoon."

"Allow me to show you the piece de resistance, Jane," Johnny said, removing the cloth covering the object on the tray. This revealed a quite extraordinary looking piece of apparatus. Jane stared at it. She recognised it immediately as the game's most famous component – its mousetrap – albeit in an improvised form. Its tiny blue plastic wheel, inside its yellow frame, attached by an axle to its plastic yellow plank, was still there, as was the lever, and the pole where the cage would normally be balanced, although this was missing. As an added extra, a series of cotton threads ran from the wheel, around the pole and from there to the pole's circular base.

Johnny picked up the wastepaper bin and carefully positioned it upside down over the pole, so that part of its rim was on the table, and part held aloft by the lever. "Something the size of a miniature washing basket isn't going to trap a mouse, is it?" Johnny said, referring to the game's original part.

"And this is?" Jane questioned. Even with this twist, she still had absolutely no idea how this was going to work.

Johnny ignored her. "You will have noticed thread," he said, gently touching one of the threads. "Mouse smells the bait, and pushes his way through the threads. But watch what happens when he does." He pressed the thread, and as he did, it tightened along its length. This caused the plank to lower, the wheel to turn and the lever to rise, which in turn released the bin to fall over the plastic mouse grazing below, and the rest of the game to collapse spectacularly. Despite this, the bin remained in place, trapping the mouse.

"Mousetrap!" both Johnny and Jack yelled simultaneously, high-fiving each other.

Jane didn't know what to say.

"We'll set it up in the summerhouse for you. I am quietly confident the pesky little critter will be in our hands by morning," Johnny said, rubbing his hands together and giving another mock laugh.

Jane couldn't see for the life of her how any of this was going to work, but it had given her enormous entertainment, and more importantly had bought Johnny and Jack closer together.

CHAPTER SEVEN

The Case of the Sister Behaving Strangely

Leaving the boys setting the trap, Jane returned to her study. Another e-mail had arrived in her absence.

'It was my husband's idea to get in touch,' the e-mail from Lucy Erpingham's sister Jodie Narbade, began. After describing the evening of Lucy's sudden departure from her house, which Jane read with fascination, Jodie continued. 'I'm certain she was about to tell me something but what I just don't know. We've hardly spoken since. We used to be such a close family, in and out of each other's houses, but we've hardly seen her for months. There's always some excuse why she can't see us. We used to speak on the phone every day, but she hasn't called me since then. She doesn't return calls, she pretends she's not in when we call round, when we know she is. She even pretended not to see our mum in the street the other day. You can imagine how upset Mum was.

'I've even turned up at her office to ask her what was going on, but she just turns it into a joke, telling me nothing is wrong, I'm overreacting, she's just been busy, she'll be in touch soon. Then nothing. If that wasn't weird enough, she's spending money like water. I know, because people are telling me. She's always liked the good things in life, what eighteen-year-old girl doesn't? But it's like she's gone crazy – buying everything she sees. She's been seen all over town in expensive clothes shops, in nightclubs and restaurants. I know for a fact she's bought a new sports car and had her teeth whitened and I'm told she's had a boob job. She only works in local government. She hasn't got the money for it. She hasn't got a rich boyfriend, as far as she's letting on. My husband thinks she's either got herself a married sugar daddy or gone on the game, and that's why she's avoiding us. I hope to God she hasn't. She was certainly being a bit secretive about this new man at work.

Things can't carry on like this. It's driving both me and Mum nuts, not knowing what's happening. I want you to follow her and find out what's going on.'

Jane understood, and even shared Jodie's concern for eighteen-year-old Lucy. She stared out of the window, unsure whether to accept or not. She already had two cases to keep her busy – although one wasn't going to start for a fortnight. Who knew – she might stumble across something in the course of her investigations which would help her with her search for Johnny's father. It had happened before. It might happen again. Also it sounded interesting. She accepted the case.

'When did all the spending start?' she asked.

'Don't know exactly. It may have started months ago, for all I know.'

'Were you arguing about anything, when you were interrupted by your neighbour? It's important I know everything.'

'No. Not at all. We were having a sisterly gossip, like I said. It's like she was suddenly invaded by body snatchers or something. She used to be a homely, family-centered girl. My husband thinks she was about to make some big confession about something – all that needing somebody to confide in business – but by the time I'd got back she'd lost her nerve and done a runner, and now she's too scared to spill the beans. I'm sure it's something to do with this bloke at work she was talking about. Maybe he's stopping her from seeing us?'

'Maybe you could send me a photograph, and any other details I'm likely to need, such as her address, workplace, mobile telephone number and daily routine?' Jane asked.

'Will do. Anything you don't get from me you'll find online. She must be on every social networking site going and she is not that good at setting her security settings. Please find out what's going on. I can't sleep at night over this. I can't help unless I know what's going on.'

The e-mail ended with plaintiff words: 'She's only 18!'

Jane spent the next few hours reading up on her subject. The photographs which Lucy Erpingham had posted of herself on-line, showed a young, short, plump, smiling woman with fair hair and a large cleavage, proudly exposed in every photograph. Lucy listed her interests as: 'spending time with me mates' 'having a laugh' 'spending money' 'shopping' 'eatin'' & drinkin'' 'acting on impulse'. She listed her favourite foods as salted potato crisps, green Thai chicken curry and chocolate ice-cream. She liked wine and coffee, but not water. Jane hadn't heard of any of Lucy's favourite bands or her favourite TV shows. Under things she hated, Lucy had written: 'getting up b4 eleven' 'dandruff' 'being on my own' 'not being able to buy everything I want!!'

Judging from what Jane had just read, Lucy seemed be a perfectly normal teenager. Jane did notice one thing, though. Lucy's social networking site hadn't been updated for months.

CHAPTER EIGHT

Think Out of the Box

I

The next morning, Jane tentatively opened the door of her summerhouse. Chaos greeted her. It was as though a demolition derby had taken place inside her summerhouse. The hinged door to the toy box remained wide open, but the grain inside was gone. In its fury to escape the Inescapable Box, the mouse had eaten through the tape and glue holding it together and it lay in pieces. The cistern lay on its side. Cardboard and plastic littered the floor. The mouse had worked his way across the room, eating whatever he found, before pushing, climbing or gnawing his way out of anything he ended up trapped inside. The mouse trap was in pieces – the threads snapped or gnawed through. Only the bin remained upright, having fallen over the pole. Fur, scattered grain, mouse droppings and a few mouse footprints surrounded it. The mouse himself though, was nowhere to be seen. Without thinking, Jane picked up the bin to see what was underneath. It was the mouse. He gave a squeak, she also. She tried to cover him with the bin again, but again he was too quick for her. This time, however, instead of running for cover behind the bookshelf, he ran out of the open door. She hurried after him and saw him running across the lawn, and disappearing through the hedge at the back. She couldn't believe it. Johnny's trap had worked. Her foe had gone. After gathering her thoughts, she returned indoors to fetch her dustbin and brush.

After clearing up after the mouse, she deposited the mess in her wheelie bin, making a mental note to buy her neighbours a new game of *Mousetrap*. Jack must have heard her because he poked his head over the fence and asked, "Did it work? Did we catch the mouse?"

"We did, but I let him slip from my grasp. He was last seen heading north."

"If he comes back, you know where we are," Jack said, wandering off to the kick a football against the wall.

Jane returned indoors to text Johnny. One task may have been completed, but Jane still had many others to do.

'Do you mind if I call your father's half-sister, Stella? She may know something helpful?' she asked.

Johnny, sat at the kitchen table with the job-page spread open in front of him, replied immediately – 'I don't mind, no, and she'll soon tell you if she does.'

Upon receiving the go-ahead Jane called Stella, but got her answer phone. She left a message, explaining who she was, and why she was calling. She could do little more, until and unless Stella returned the call. She went to pack, for her stakeout of Lucy Erpingham was to start the next day.

II

Johnny studied the job's page.

The whereabouts of his missing father wasn't the only thing on his mind. Johnny needed money, and he needed it badly. He wanted to take Charity away skiing, to try and make amends, but he was skint. What money he hadn't used up in travelling to South America, he'd used to buy his ticket home. He'd sold all his possessions. He'd even swapped his motorbike for a van so he could go back to work as a tree surgeon. He was sure work there would slowly pick up, but not quickly enough for him to take Charity skiing. He knew Jane would lend him the money, but he didn't want to borrow it. He wanted to show Charity and Jack that he really had changed by earning it himself. He studied the job's page again. If he were to take any of these jobs, it would take him months to raise the money he needed. He closed the paper. Think laterally, he said to himself. Think out of the box. Box! he said, jumping to his feet and running out of the house towards his shed at the end of the garden.

CHAPTER NINE

Dabney Farm

I

At half-past six in the evening, a motorist stopped by the side of the Southstoft Road to read the hand-painted sandwich board Johnny wore around his neck. This car was the first stop in an hour. The driver read the sign out loud, *"Need money. Will do (nearly) anything to earn it,"* then asked snidely, "Got debts have you?"

"Nothing like that, mate," Johnny replied. "Need to make it up to the girlfriend. Want to take her skiing."

"Kick you out, did she?" the driver asked.

"Yeah, then she let me back in again, and I want to make sure she lets me stay."

The driver burst out laughing. "I like your attitude, son," he said. "I run Dabney Farm. Two of our temporary workers have gone sick. I can give you a night's work, if you want it. It's not easy work though, and I can't pay you no more than the minimum."

Johnny leaned up to the car window: "Cash?" he asked.

II

"She's a bit energetic," Johnny said of a young woman exercising in the field, turning to look at her out of the back windscreen. The land was flat for miles – green, undulating, stretched out below a sky as empty as the landscape below it. Even though it was growing dark, and he couldn't see anyone else in the field, the young woman was turning round and round in a circle, her arms outstretched.

"She don't approve of Dabney farm. She wanted me to give her my chickens but I refused so she's trying to put a hex on the place."

"A what?" Johnny said, just as the girl fell over. "Think we should go back – make sure she's okay?" he asked.

"Na. Tan't nothing wrong with her but one too many magic mushrooms! Here we are, Dabney Farm," the farm's owner said of the row of enormous corrugated iron buildings they were driving towards, each about the size of ten football fields, which lit up the night sky.

"You're doing okay for yourself," Johnny said, wondering where he'd gone wrong in life.

"I'm an opportunist me. Bought half a broiler unit twenty years ago now and I ain't never looked back. Chickens – can't make enough of them – but where there's chickens, there's chicken poo."

"Don't need to ask what my job is, then?"

Within ten minutes of arriving at the farm, Johnny was waiting outside the empty broiler unit he'd been assigned to scrub out, dressed in wellington boots, a rubber apron, and elbow-length rubber gloves. A head scarf was tied around his hair, over which he wore a plastic cap. He and the other temporary workers gathered around the foreman.

"High-pressure water's been spraying down the unit for weeks now," the foreman explained. "We call that phase one. But phase one don't get everything. Takes an old-fashioned scrubbing brush to do that. We call that phase two. That's you lot!" He pressed the remote control in his hand and the unit's doors swung open, revealing a river of sawdust, feathers and chicken poo running down the unit's walls and over its the floor. "In you go my lovelies," he said.

The smell made Johnny step back. Not so his colleagues. Unfazed by sight or smell, each ambled into the unit. Johnny reluctantly followed them. He took his cue from them, scraping away anything still left on the perches and walls. The job wasn't hard – everything came away easily – just unpleasant. Particularly the smell. It was vile, clawing. He couldn't stand it. He threw down his brush and ran outside to get some fresh air.

"Time out's deducted from your wages," the foreman said, upon his return.

"What!" Johnny said, spinning around. The sharpness in his movement caused him to slip and fall over backwards into the slimy mixture of muddy water, feathers, sawdust, and poop. He got to his feet again, soaked through from the putrid sludge.

"You can go and clear up if you like, but it'll be another deduction," the foreman informed him.

"I'll stay."

"That wall, over there," the foreman instructed.

Johnny joined some others in scrubbing down the enormous eastern wall of the barn. He extended the handle on his scrubbing brush until it was tall enough to reach to the top of the wall and began scrubbing. Great job you've landed yourself here, mate – he thought to himself – cleaning chicken shit off a tin can!

By the time break time arrived, every part of his body ached, he was ravenously hungry, covered from head to toe in a mixture of poo and straw, and was coughing furiously, not that this prevented him from accepting a cigarette from a workmate. He smoked it on the way to the shower block, where he cleaned up as best he could. From there he quickly made his way to the staff canteen, to discover he only had enough money on him to buy two apples and a cup of tea for his evening meal, unless he wanted his wages deducted by the cost of something better. He also learned that meal breaks were unpaid for temporary workers. Minutes later, an apple in each pocket, he was inside another huge corrugated iron barn.

This unit was the size of a mere five football pitches. A waist-high conveyor belt carried partially-feathered chicken carcasses slowly across the room. Johnny stood behind it, dressed this time in a white overall, face mask, and plastic gloves. At the other end of the barn, people fed unplucked chickens into a machine from which they emerged moments later, freshly plucked, except the wings.

"The machine can't get the wing feathers," the foreman explained. "Also you'll find that every now and then an unplucked chicken gets through. Pluck anything with feathers anywhere on it and put it up there." The foreman pointed to an overhead conveyor belt from which plucked carcasses hung.

The smell inside this unit was almost as bad as the smell inside the other unit. The air was full of feathers, and despite the face mask, Johnny coughed even more than he had when cleaning out the chicken coup. He was also shivering, and his hands turning blue.

"Yeah we have to keep the place as cold as we can. We don't want the chickens barbecuing do we?" the foreman said. "We expect fifteen an hour, and any where the skin's torn will be a deduction from your wages, 'cos we get less for them," he explained, picking up a chicken to show Johnny how to pluck it. "See how you get on."

Johnny didn't get on very well. He tried to keep up with the others, but they were all much quicker than him. He glanced to his right and then his left. For some reason, the feathers on his chickens didn't seem to come out as easily as the feathers of the chickens being plucked on either side of him. If he didn't tug hard enough, the feathers didn't come out, but if he tugged too hard, he risked tearing the skin and being docked money.

"You have to pull them out at an angle," a girl standing next to him explained. "See?" she said, twisting a chicken in one direction, and deftly plucking out its feathers in another. But Johnny didn't see. He tried, but twist and pull as he did, the feathers still refused to come out. The cold wasn't helping. It was like trying to work in a freezer. By the next break time, he'd only managed to pluck six chickens, two of which were only good enough to be made into pies. He soon found himself on packing duty, struggling to keep awake and it wasn't even two a.m.

III

"That had to be the worst job I've ever done!" he said to Charity the next morning, as he stretched out in the bath tub. "I'm twenty-nine and feel ninety-eight. I've got frostbite in my fingers. I can hardly move. And there was me thinking I'd get offered work as a naked bartender or something equally upmarket…"

"I don't think Failsham has bars like that, Johnny."

He ignored her and continued, "… instead of which I end up working from six p.m. to six a.m. – on a Sunday – without a break or a meal, for a pittance – less deductions! And they didn't even want me back."

Charity, sat on the toilet seat, giggled.

"I'm glad you find it so funny." He wriggled his toes. "They're about the only part of me which still moves." He bit into the last slice of the family-sized pizza he'd returned home with.

"You don't need to do this, Johnny."

"I'm going to earn enough to take you skiing if it kills me, darlin'."

"Well in that case there's only one thing for it."

"What?"

"Back to the sandwich board!"

CHAPTER TEN

Lucy Erpingham

Lucy caught the bus to work from the bus stop outside the apartment block where she lived and therefore Jane began her surveillance of Lucy Erpingham by parking near the girl's apartment block. She made her way to Lucy's bus stop on foot, at eight o'clock, Monday morning.

Lucy needed to catch the eight twenty bus to be on time for work, but on the first morning of the stake-out, a flustered-looking Lucy didn't leave her apartment block until gone nine. Unfortunately for Lucy, she wasn't the only thing running late that morning. The late running of the bus left Lucy looking at her watch and stamping her feet, whilst muttering, "Come on! Come on! I'm going to be late! I'm behind on my flexi already!" over and over again, much to the amusement of her fellow passengers.

Jane watched this from the end of the bus queue. She had to resist the temptation to laugh out loud, when Lucy telephoned her office to explain she was running late because, "The stupid bus hasn't turned up again!"

By the end of the week, Jane would be left wondering why on earth Lucy even attempted to get to work for nine a.m.

because not a day seemed to go by when Lucy managed to reach her office before ten. Not that her tardiness seemed to cause Lucy much concern. Quite the contrary. Even when she got off the bus, Lucy did not make her way straight to her office, instead she dawdled along the High Street, finding the time to window-shop, and purchase a breakfast muffin and a latté from a local deli. Jane wondered why nobody in the office asked her how it was she managed to find time to stop off at a coffee shop to purchase breakfast, when she was already late for work?

It was almost ten o'clock when Lucy entered the modern office block, where she worked. Lucy's office was open-plan, and her desk was near a large window on the ground floor, which overlooked the High Street. This conveniently allowed Jane to sit on a park bench quite near the office, from where she could watch Lucy at her desk, from a discreet distance.

From her surveillance point, Jane could see photos on Lucy's desk. From what she could tell, these looked like photos of the family Lucy had suddenly cut out of her life. Jane spent the morning watching Lucy sitting in front of a computer screen, tapping away at a keyboard. Her job, Jane assumed, must involve providing some type of advice to customers, because she wore a headphone and seemed to spend most of her time speaking into it. Lucy took the occasional short breaks away from her desk, but spent most of the morning sitting at it, working diligently. That first day, Lucy spent a shortened lunch break with colleagues in a bistro next to the office. Jane was able to loiter outside the bistro long enough to see Lucy take a large slurp from a glass of white wine, whilst eating from a plate of chips topped with melted cheese. Jane herself ate a packed lunch in her car.

When Jane returned to the park bench opposite the office, Lucy was already back at her desk. Her afternoon seemed to pass in much the same way as the morning, except that this time much more time was spent away from her desk and much more time was spent standing at a colleague desk, arms folded, laughing and joking. That the lunchtime wine had obviously made her colleagues' small talk highly amusing.

Lucy's working day ended at six p.m. In the end, she'd managed to work an eight hour shift. Jane was ready to call it a day. She had spent most of the time sitting at a park bench, either reading a newspaper and looking at her watch impatiently (as though waiting for somebody) or knitting. Jane was certain she must have been captured on a CCTV camera, but hoped her behaviour would be put down as lonely/eccentric. This was one of the advantages of age. Unusual behaviour was put down to something pitiful, rather than threatening or concerning. Lucy had not seemed to notice Jane sat there, but Jane knew she could not spend the rest of the week sat at the same park bench, staring into the office window, without either Lucy herself, or one of her colleagues, noticing her and becoming suspicious. She'd have to move somewhere else.

Jane may have been ready to go home, but for Lucy, the day was just starting; and before long, Jane was sitting alone at a table in a wine bar, with a coffee in front of her, whilst three tables away, Lucy and her colleagues were beginning their evening by ordering three bottles of wine. Jane noticed the wine was paid for by Lucy on Lucy's credit card. Jane eventually left the tiddly girls noisily piling into an Indian restaurant at eleven o'clock at night. No wonder she's late for work in the mornings. Jane thought, letting herself into her car.

The next day Lucy arrived for work at just before ten in the morning. Jane sat on a different park bench, making herself as comfortable as possible, this time with the help of an inflatable cushion and pretended to engross herself in a book, from which she looked up now and then to ensure Lucy was still at her desk. The second day of her surveillance seemed only to differ from the first, in that Lucy spent her lunch hour in a small family-run boutique, down the road from the office.

The busy high street, on which Lucy's office was located, contained many such shops, which ranged from tiny boutiques to large national chains. Jane watched Lucy try on almost every jacket in the shop, while Jane pretended to be interested in some dresses on a rail. Now and then she selected one and held it up against herself. The assistant watching her had stopped smiling. Jane was going to have to either buy something, or leave the shop. She chose the latter, leaving a full twenty minutes before Lucy did. When Lucy left the store, she did so clutching a very large store bag, leaving Jane to wonder which jacket she'd eventually bought. No doubt she'd find out when Lucy returned to the office as she would undoubtedly end up showing the purchased item to her colleagues, as was the way with almost any woman who had purchased something nice and new in her lunch hour. On the way back to the office, Lucy popped into a sandwich bar and bought herself some lunch.

After quickly modelling her new jacket for her colleagues, she returned to work, eating her lunch at her desk between calls, watched by Jane, now eating her own lunch.

Lucy caught the twenty past six bus home. Lucy climbed up to the upper deck, while Jane remained on the lower deck.

Unseen by Lucy, Jane followed her off the bus. On the way to her apartment block, Lucy stopped off to buy herself a takeaway pizza. This girl's diet is appalling, Jane thought to herself disapprovingly, as Lucy returned to her apartment carrying the large pizza box in one hand, and clutching her shopping bag in the other. Jane suspected that Lucy wouldn't be enjoying a quiet night in. She had a sinking feeling that it was going to be another long night. She decided to wait to see if Lucy reappeared. As she had no idea how long this would be, she took herself off to a local restaurant and ordered some soup and a salad.

Lucy eventually left her flat again dressed up for a night out in a short tight black dress, and a pair of black platform sandals, which Jane eyed rather jealously. She herself wore a pair of black flat lace-ups. While she no longer loathed such footwear as much as she had done when she was Lucy's age, she still loved heels – the higher, the better. Unfortunately, a combination of her age, sciatica, and her new line of business, meant she rarely wore them anymore, much as she adored them.

Based on her outfit and pizza supper, Jane guessed Lucy was going to a nightclub, rather than a restaurant. Lucy jumped on board the bus, followed by Jane. Lucy sat on the lower deck, with Jane two rows behind her. Lucy spent the entire journey texting, looking up only long enough to press the STOP BUS bell. Jane was the last to disembark. Lucy was so busy texting that she nearly walked past the nightclub she was going to. Three girls, all about the same age as Lucy, already in the queue forming outside the nightclub, had to shout her name out as she went past: "Lucy!" they yelled. She stopped dead in her tracks, realised her mistake, and hurried over to join them in the queue. All shrieked with laughter at Lucy's absent-mindedness.

Jane stopped someway back and pretended to window-shop. It was still quite early and the queue outside the club was quite short. It wouldn't be long before Lucy and her friends would be inside. Jane had no intention of following them. There was no way a woman in her sixties could blend into the background of a nightclub, even one dressed in black slacks and a polo neck jumper, however dark it was. Jane would need to think of something else. She spotted a gastro-pub on the other side of the road from the nightclub. The pub was one of a well-known national chain and was family orientated, although at that moment Jane could only see young people inside. Nonetheless, she made her way there, to sit at the window seat with a coffee and a paper in front of her. She could kill an hour or five in relative anonymity – although she may need to drink a lot of coffee.

To Jane's relief (and possibly because it was a work night) Lucy eventually left the club before eleven. She was clearly the worse for wear. Lucy was still in the company of her friends. Jane watched the group stagger to a taxi rank. The girls kissed each other goodbye and each got into a taxi alone. Jane could not be certain where Lucy was going, but the taxi did leave in the direction of Lucy's flat. It was too late to follow her now. Jane would have to leave it at that and return home.

Thus ended the second day of her surveillance of Lucy. So far she had little to report, other than there didn't seem to be a sugar daddy in sight, not that she'd seen, anyway.

The third day of Jane's surveillance was not dissimilar from the previous two days, except that the evening was spent with Jane sitting by herself in the corner of a champagne bar, nursing a solitary glass of sparkling white wine, watching Lucy and her colleagues swill champagne. Champagne which, Jane noticed, was paid for by Lucy. She even heard Lucy say, "No, it's on me. I want to. Spending money makes me happy."

Jane couldn't help noticing that Lucy was starting to look as tired as Jane herself was feeling. Thankfully the evening ended at a relatively civilised hour, with Lucy returning home alone just after half past eleven in the evening.

Friday night was spent in a wine bar next to Lucy's apartment block. As always, Lucy was surrounded by other young people and the alcohol flowed freely, mostly paid for by Lucy again. The evening ended with Lucy and her friends returning to Lucy's flat, after a visit to a kebab shop.

It was almost the end of her first week's surveillance, and all Jane had learnt about Lucy was that she spent too much money, ate badly and burned the candle at both ends – so far nothing atypical for an eighteen year old girl; and nothing to explain the unusual rift with her family.

CHAPTER ELEVEN

Jill

I

Jane began her weekend surveillance of Lucy's flat quite early on Saturday morning. She managed to find a free parking space on the opposite side of the road from the apartment block. Lucy's apartment was in darkness, her curtains drawn. As Jane had no idea when Lucy was likely to put in an appearance (although she suspected it wouldn't be early), she'd brought with her a book, a thermos flask of coffee, and some sandwiches. She settled herself down for the wait.

Lucy's apartment remained in darkness for the entire morning. The curtains remained drawn until past lunchtime, but she didn't leave the apartment for another hour. From the car, Jane watched Lucy walk along the high street and into a nail bar. Another long wait, Jane thought. She took the opportunity to step out of the car and stretch her legs with a walk to the public toilets and back.

Lucy emerged from the nail bar a couple of hours later, sporting a set of new, bright red nails. She'd also had her hair tinted and blow-dried into a fashionable bob. She must be going out for the evening again. Good for her, thought Jane who'd enjoyed plenty of late nights herself when she'd still been Lucy's age, and didn't begrudge any young person doing the same. On her way back to her flat, Lucy called briefly into a local grocery store and left it not much later, clutching a shopping bag of groceries. These she carried back inside her apartment block. As Jane watched her, she wondered if she'd be able to follow her that evening.

Bearing in mind the time it normally took Lucy to get ready, Jane judged she had enough time to visit a nearby cafe and eat a light supper there.

At about eight o'clock, Lucy emerged from her apartment block and climbed into a waiting taxi, wearing a short, blue, cut-away dress, high-heeled silver sandals, and holding a beautifully wrapped parcel. A balloon with the words, 'Happy 19th Birthday!' emblazoned on it, bobbed in the air behind her, attached by a piece of string to her silver handbag. When the taxi left Jane followed it. The journey didn't take long. The taxi pulled up outside a local hotel and Lucy got out. While Lucy walked into the hotel, Jane parked. By the time she got back to the hotel, Lucy had disappeared. A sign in the hotel lobby told Jane the hotel's conference room had been booked for a private party. She spent some minutes in the lobby, watching other young girls arriving for the party, carrying birthday presents and cards.

All this reminded Jane of the sister she'd lost – Jill. Jill died a few weeks before her nineteenth birthday and now all Jane could see was the number nineteen: 19 Today! Happy 19th! 19! 19! 19! It was too much to bear. The pain of her loss came flooding back as it did from time to time, in a tide of grief so searing she had no choice but to let the tears come. She didn't want to walk through the streets in tears, or sit sobbing in her car in a car park, she needed somewhere where she could be alone, where people weren't going to stop to ask if she was all right.

She walked over to the reception desk, managing to hold the tears back as she booked a room. She contained herself while she took the escalator to it, but once through the door, she collapsed in tears.

'Girl pillion thrown to death after collision between motorbike and lorry!' the newspapers reported.

She would always remember her poor mother screaming,

"She wasn't a girl pillion – she was my daughter!"

Decades may had passed since her sister's death, yet not a day went by when Jane didn't re-live the moment her father sat on the end of her bed to break the news to her. She still found it impossible to talk about. She hadn't even been able to talk to Hugh about it, other than to tell him what had happened. She still had the present she'd bought for Jill – a hard backed Navy blue diary – on which she'd written,

'To Jill,

Happy 19th

Your loving sister, Jane'

on its inside cover, before wrapping it up and putting the present inside a plastic bag for safekeeping.

The wrapped present, still in its plastic bag, now lay in an empty shoebox in the bottom drawer of her writing bureau. Since the day she had put the diary inside its box, not once had she taken it out, nor would she ever. To this day, she could not bear to hold the present in her hands, and she knew she wouldn't ever be able to unwrap it, open it, and read her own words written there, but she would never part with it either.

II

Jane awoke abruptly, having fallen asleep. She glanced at her watch. Good heavens – it was the early hours of the morning. How could she have been so remiss? Lucy could have left the party with any one.

She hurried downstairs to the hotel's reception, just as the party ended, and its guests, including Lucy, piled out of the conference room, each as drunk as the other. The girls noisily bid the birthday girl goodbye on the steps of the hotel, and climbed into waiting taxis. Jane hurried back to her car.

She managed to beat the taxi to Lucy's apartment block, and arrived in time to see Lucy, the last in the taxi, stagger out of the car and into her apartment block. Jane waited until the lights in her apartment went out, before tilting her car seat back and drifting off to sleep.

She awoke at eleven a.m. Lucy's apartment was still in darkness, curtains drawn. Jane got out of the car. She was rather stiff. As Lucy wasn't likely to emerge from her apartment block much before midday, Jane decided to go for a walk to loosen up, and buy herself some breakfast and a paper. She returned to her car with both, and continued her stake-out. It had turned half-past one when Lucy eventually stepped out of her front door.

Lucy drove her new car to the local shopping mall, where she spent the afternoon going from shop to shop, purchasing something in every store, with Jane trailing after her, marvelling at her ability to shop without stopping or dropping. In one shop, Lucy tried on every single pair of jeans, left without buying anything, returning minutes later to purchase three pairs of jeans in the same style but different colours. Jane hadn't thought there was anyone who enjoyed clothes shopping more than she, but even she was amazed by Lucy's ability to spend money. By her calculations, based on only one week's observation of Lucy, if she kept shopping at this rate, she'd soon own more clothes than she'd be able to wear in a life-time, even if she only wore them once. What does she do with all these unwanted purchases, Jane wondered. Were they languishing in the back of her wardrobe? Or did Lucy actually spend her time in the office selling her unwanted purchases on-line? At that moment, a tannoy announced that as it was four p.m., the shopping mall was closing.

While the shops started to close up for the day, those in the shopping centre – mostly groups of friends or family members – began to drift out. Jane continued to watch Lucy, beginning to get her first real feel of the girl since she'd begun her surveillance of her. It was abundantly obvious that Lucy did not wish to leave the shopping centre. She looked vulnerable and even rather panic-stricken. Left with no choice, Lucy left the store to return to her car with her shopping. She didn't get into the car though. She opened it and threw her shopping bags onto its back seat, locked the car again, then made her way out of the car park and over towards a small park on one side of the shopping mall, followed at a safe distance by Jane.

On the way there, Lucy stopped off to buy four extra large burgers and fries, two bags of doughnuts, a bottle of fizzy drink, and a coffee. More junk food, Jane thought, with a shake of the head. Carrying the food in two brown paper bags, Lucy crossed the park in the direction of an alcove created by a hedge and some trees. Jane continued to follow her, staying some way behind. When Lucy reached the semicircular alcove, she sat down on the ground there, shielded from the main park by a hedge. Jane sat down on the grass on the other side of the hedge, and unseen by Lucy, she gently parted the branches. She saw Lucy take out her provisions and lay them on the ground in front of her.

Jane watched on in mild disgust as Lucy furiously rammed, first a large mouthful of burger, then fries and doughnuts into her mouth. She ate as though she was ravenous, even angry. When she couldn't get any more food in her mouth, she slurped down fizzy orange drink and hot coffee, almost choking in her haste, only to start the frenzy of comfort eating again. The bingeing continued until there wasn't anything left to eat or drink and the wrappers had been licked clean. Lucy wiped her hand across her mouth and stared at the empty packaging in front of her for some time. "Enjoyed that did you!" she said out loud.

The tone used was so direct, that for a split second, Jane wondered if Lucy had actually seen her. But she hadn't. Lucy's comments she realised, were directed at Lucy.

"You greedy cow! Couldn't stop yourself could you? Oh no! You never can, can you? You have no self-control! You're pathetic! You're like a child in a sweet shop!" Lucy taunted herself.

Jane was amazed by the outburst she was witnessing. The comments were so critical, and spoken in such an unpleasant tone of voice that Jane wondered whether she was repeating something unpleasant that someone had once said to her. By now, Lucy was bent over, crying. In between her sobs, she asked herself the same question over and over again. "Why did you do it? Why? It hasn't made you happy, has it?"

Jane wasn't surprised to discover that happy-go-lucky Lucy was in reality rather lonely. A day like today, a lovely bright Sunday, could only serve to remind Lucy how alone she was. Most girls of her age, all her friends probably, would either be spending the day with their families or with their boyfriends. Lucy as yet didn't have a boyfriend, and she'd mysteriously cut her family out of her life for reasons that Jane was frankly no closer to establishing.

Lucy suddenly stuffed the empty packaging into the paper bags, got to her feet and walked over to a nearby paper bin, where she deposited the bags. Still sobbing and talking to herself, she walked towards the exit. Jane gave her a few minutes before she too left the park, again from a safe distance.

Lucy left the mall's car park before Jane. Jane followed Lucy to her apartment then drove home. She was worried about Lucy. As far as she could tell, she was basically a good kid, but not a particularly happy one. Lucy almost certainly wasn't working as a prostitute, and if Lucy had a Svengali-like man in her life, Jane had found no sign of him. This was a result of sorts. But it still left the question – where was she getting the money – unanswered. Was it the never-never? Did she have creditors after her? Was she about to be declared bankrupt at the grand old age of eighteen, and was it this that was causing her so much embarrassment that she'd rather not see her own family?

As Jane opened her front door, she heard the telephone ringing in the hallway. She hurried to answer it, only to spend the next ten minutes answering questions about who she was intending to vote for at the next election and why. It was during the call that an idea came to her. As soon as the call was over, Jane sat in her study and prepared a script based on a conversation she'd just had with the opinion poll company. She read the script back to herself, before telephoning Lucy's mobile phone number. After a few rings, a groggy-sounding Lucy answered. It sounded as though she'd just woken up from a nap.

"Just a courtesy call, on behalf of an opinion poll agency," Jane began, sounding rather professional, if she said so herself. "Your telephone number has been randomly selected. Your identity remains confidential, not just to myself, but also to my agency. May I take a few minutes of your time to ask you a few questions if it's not too much trouble?"

"Not at all," Lucy answered. Jane had already worked out that Lucy was an attention craving girl, and for a girl such as that, any attention, in whatever form, was better than none at all. "May I begin by asking you if you are over eighteen?" Jane began.

"I'm exactly eighteen," Lucy said yawning.

"That puts you in the eighteen - twenty-four age range," Jane said, tapping the keyboard of her computer randomly, to make it sound as though she was inputting data. "Now, as I've mentioned, this call to you was randomly generated and all the information gathered from it will remain entirely confidential, and we will not be able to trace it back to you. We will not even retain a copy of your telephone number, either. So, to repeat, your answers are completely anonymous. Neither I, nor the company I work for, have any idea who you are, nor will we be able to trace you."

Jane heard Lucy yawning, this time louder than before. Well, you have rather laboured the point, Jane, she thought to herself.

"Whatever," Lucy said, with adolescent indifference.

"My first question – how much unsecured debt do you have?"

"Dunno. Dunno what that means, do I?"

"It means, do you owe anybody money, other than a loan you may have borrowed from a bank to buy the property you live in."

"In that case, none. I rent my flat. I might buy it, though. I haven't decided."

"Do you have a bank overdraft?" Jane asked.

"Not any more."

"Do you use a credit card?"

"Certainly do," Lucy giggled. "Be lost without it, wouldn't I?"

"Can I ask if you pay your card balance off at the end of each month?"

"I do now."

"How much would you say you spend each month on non-vital items?" Jane asked.

"You mean like clothes and stuff?"

"Yes," Jane answered.

"Dunno, a few hundred, something like that."

And the rest, Jane thought. "To recap. You do not have a mortgage, you do not have any debt, you do use a credit card, but you pay it off at the end of each month, and you spend hundreds each month on non-essential items, in addition to your expenditure on essential items?"

"That's right. I'm my own woman. Kept by no one!"

Lucy sounded a little smug. Ordinarily, Jane would have been rather impressed by hearing a woman of Lucy's age make such a statement, but in this case, it left her feeling more than alarmed. "Oh, I see, so you earn quite a lot, then?" she said.

"Not really. I just got lucky recently, that's all."

Really? Jane thought to herself. How exactly?

"Do you mean you inherited some money?" she asked.

Jane knew this was most unlikely, for surely Jodie also would have inherited, or at least known about it.

"Sort of like an inheritance, but not an inheritance, if you know what I mean?" Lucy answered.

Jane didn't.

"Can I ask what you mean by that?"

"No you bleedin' well can't, Lady! You got any more questions or can I get back to sleep?"

"I think I've asked you everything. You've been most kind. Most kind."

Jane replaced the receiver and sat back in her chair. She replayed Lucy's words in her mind: I just got lucky recently. Sort of like an inheritance, but not an inheritance, if you know what I mean?

Lucy's words raised a whole plethora of possibilities. Jane realised she was going to have to get a hold of a bank statement, and check Lucy's story out before she could do anything else. Unfortunately, she could only think of one way to do this – rummaging through Lucy's rubbish bags – and probably the rubbish bags of half of Lucy's apartment block, as well.

CHAPTER TWELVE

Stella Barnes

No sooner did her call to Lucy end, than her phone rang again. This time the caller was Pete Lambert's half-sister, Stella Barnes.

"Johnny wants to know where Pete is?" Stella said, once Jane had explained the reason for her call. "Bloody hell! After all this time! I'm not sure I can help you very much. I haven't seen Pete since the day he left Johnny's mum, Sue. She rang me and started screaming down the phone that Pete was leaving her. I ran from my place to hers – they only lived round the corner. Time I got there, all hell had let loose. Pete and Sue were outside, along with half the street. Pete was sat astride his motorcycle. Sue was holding the little-un, screaming at him not to leave. The kiddie was howling. One of their neighbours was trying to make him see sense. I ran up to Pete and asked him what the hell he thought he was doing, leaving his wife and kid. He looked straight through me, like I wasn't even there, fastened his helmet and roared off, like he was going to work or somewhere. Apart from a letter I haven't seen or heard from him to this day forth."

"Letter?" Jane asked.

"Yeah, it arrived about a year or so after he left, maybe longer. I hadn't heard a word from him, nor had Sue, since the day he went, then out of the blue this letter from him dropped on my mat. Inside was this handwritten note. It was definitely his handwriting. It was typical Pete – 'Meet me in Gote, 27th, 5.30 in the Fleet, Pete' – nothing more. At first I didn't know where Gote was – I had to look it up on a map. Turns out, it wasn't that far away from where we were living. I didn't tell Sue, because I thought it more likely than not he wouldn't show, which turned out to be the case. I couldn't even find anywhere called the Fleet, but someone there told me it was the old name for the Hare and Hounds, so I went there. I got there before five and I stayed until after closing time, but needless to say, he didn't show. He didn't specify the month, but the letter arrived on the twentieth, I remember that. Like the mug I am, I even went back the next month, but the same thing happened. Typical Pete – the hours of my life I've wasted waiting for him not to show.

"I'm just glad I didn't tell Sue. Whenever I saw her she asked me if I'd heard from him. She was always convinced I knew where he was, but I didn't. I remember bumping into her in the street a little later. First thing she said to me, 'Have you heard from Pete?' I said I hadn't. She walked away without saying anything. I felt so sorry for her. Being the idiot I am, I kept going back to Gore to see if I could find him, but I never did. I looked his name up in the phone book and everything, but I never found a trace of him.

"From that day to this I've heard nothing from him. I have no idea where he could be. I don't even know if he's still alive.

It beats me why Johnny would want to see him again 'cept to punch his lights out," she said.

"Did he ever share any secret dreams with you that he had, which might shed some light on where he might have gone after he left Johnny's mother?" Jane asked.

"He was full of bullshit that one. He was going to join the army, move to the Costa Del Sol, open a pub on the South Coast, a motorcycle repair shop, you name it, he was going to do it. Even if he did any of those things, I can't believe he'd have stuck at it for very long. Pete couldn't stick at anything that was the problem."

"Did he have any nicknames or 'nom de guerres' he liked to be known as, that you can remember?" Jane asked. She was running out of ideas.

"None," Stella said. "Not that I can think of, sorry."

Jane came off the phone, feeling frustrated and disappointed in her failure to help Johnny. "Dammit!" she said out loud. "Dammit! Dammit!"

CHAPTER THIRTEEN

The Bin Woman

At two in the morning, Jane walked over to the two communal waste disposal bins, at the rear of Lucy's apartment block, wearing a dark blue overall, a black woollen hat, yellow rubber gloves and a face mask. She wasn't sure what she'd say if the police caught her. She'd have to hope they didn't.

Each wheelie bin held dozens of rubbish bags. With a torch in one hand, Jane pushed open the lid of a bin, and removed one of the bags. Before she opened it, she ripped off a black plastic bag from a roll she'd brought with her and, to stop rubbish from spilling everywhere, she put the bag she'd just retrieved from the wheelie bin inside it. She cut open the rubbish bag using a penknife. She searched through the rubbish until she found an envelope addressed to one of Lucy's neighbours. She tied the bag up and put it to one side. She removed another bag – from another neighbour. She carried on, opening bag after bag. Most of the next hour was taken up with her rummaging through other people's rubbish. Her face mask did little to stop the smell, but hopefully it would stop her from inhaling something noxious. In her search she came across some quite extraordinary items: unopened cans, unworn clothing still in packaging, electrical goods still in their boxes, an unbroken kitchen drawer, and in one bag, a beautiful tiffany necklace still in its box, which Jane decided she would give to a charity shop. The residents of the block had very different personality types, judging by the contents of their rubbish bags. Some of the residents clearly sorted their rubbish carefully into recyclable and non-recyclable items, others seemed to discard everything, recyclable or not, including most of their unopened weekly food shopping. Some shredded confidential paperwork, others weren't concerned. Some seemed to wash cartons before throwing them out, others didn't bother.

Jane glanced at her watch. Time was flying by, yet she'd only looked through one of the bins, with little to show for it. This summed up the case to date, she thought. As quickly as she could, she put the rubbish sacks back in the bin and closed the lid. At the second bin she repeated the process again. This time it was more fruitful. She found Lucy's rubbish in the third black plastic bag she ripped into – she recognised the pizza box. She rummaged through the rubbish bag until she came across a stained, soggy credit card statement. A little further down she found a damp bank statement. Neither had been shredded. She put both in freezer bags, then hurled the black refuse bag, facemask and the rubber gloves into the bin and returned to her car. Once home, she put the statements in her airing cupboard to dry out, and went to bed.

The next morning, she studied the dried-out statements. They confirmed that Lucy was spending a lot of money – hardly a surprise. What was more of a surprise though was the tens of thousands of pounds in Lucy's bank account. Nothing on the bank statement indicated where this money had come from.

It certainly wasn't from the modest, regular salary which was being paid into her account every month. She was certainly spending it at quite a rate, though. Jane put the bank statement down, and re-read the credit card statement. Lucy had spent close to a thousand pounds that month, as she had the month before. This balance, and the balance from the month before, had both been paid in full, which confirmed what Lucy had told her.

Jane looked at the bank statement again. One thing was clear – the money in Lucy's bank account wasn't being replenished at anything like the rate at which it was being spent. Jane could only speculate how Lucy had come by so much money. A number of solutions presented themselves to her: maybe she'd checked her lottery numbers when her sister was helping the neighbour, found she'd won and scarpered, rather than feeling obliged to share it. Maybe she'd checked her bank account, discovered the bank had paid some money into her account they shouldn't have done, and knowing her sister would tell her to pay it back, left abruptly. Or maybe there was a man around after all, paying money into her account in exchange for something. The man at work? Maybe this is what she'd been about to confess that evening at Jodie's house?

Even more worrying was the possibility that she'd allowed someone to launder money through her account. Even worse, she might have simply helped herself to someone else's money when the opportunity had presented itself – her employers possibly. She might have done this alone or with others. If so, what would Lucy do when the money ran out, Jane mused. Help herself to some more? Or be pressurised into doing so? This might explain why she was still going into work every day. Questions! Questions! Questions!

The only thing Jane knew for sure is that she couldn't go back to Jodie at this stage with what she had. She needed more evidence, although how she would find that evidence, for the moment exuded her. But somehow she would, for this was exactly the kind of mystery she loved getting her teeth into.

CHAPTER FOURTEEN

Tricky Mickey

Jane's mood dipped slightly upon flinging open the summer-house door to discover the mouse had returned. She'd moved her books from the summerhouse into the conservatory for safekeeping, and covered her comfy chairs with plastic sheets, but these were ripped in places and a corner nibbled, as was a chair leg. Droppings and fur covered the floor. Any more of this Mickey and its Warfarin for you! she said darkly, returning to her cottage to fetch a dustbin and brush. On her way back she spotted Jack leaning over the garden fence. "I knew he'd come back," he said. "They home."

It wasn't long before he joined her in the summerhouse.

"Johnny sent me over with this," he said, pushing a plastic bag into her hands. Jane looked inside it. It contained human hair. Lots of it.

"It's from Charity's clients, with a bit of ours thrown in," he explained. "Mice hate it apparently. Can't stand it! Human hair, loud noises and lion dung – but we didn't think you'd want us turning up with a bag of lion dung! If you sprinkle it all over the floor, he'll scarper."

"Well, I suppose it's worth a try," Jane said sceptically.

"Johnny also suggested setting your smoke alarm off. Loud noise drives them to distraction."

"Me also," Jane said.

"Does the summerhouse have a smoke alarm?"

"It does," she said, motioning towards the ceiling.

"If you swap its batteries for ones which are almost flat, it will go off," Jack said sagely. "We're always leaving our batteries in too long. Our smoke alarm's always going off."

Living next door to them, Jane already knew this. "Swapping the batteries does seem a much better alternative to lighting a naked flame in a wooden building adjacent to a thatched cottage," she replied.

"I'll get it down for you," Jack said, jumping on a chair to remove the alarm from the ceiling. He handed it to her, saying, "Johnny's ordered a humane mouse trap for you, in case this doesn't work, but we think it will."

Jack gave her a wave before he disappeared out of the door, leaving her to stare into the bag of hair. Sprinkling human hair over her summerhouse floor probably wasn't worse than what was crawling all over it, she decided, draping a row of hair around the summerhouse walls. She tipped the remains from the bag over the floor and furniture.

Back in her kitchen, she swapped the batteries from her smoke alarm for some she had removed from her remote control the week before, after she'd had to keep turning them around and around to get the remote to work. Almost immediately the kitchen was filled with an intermittent shriek. This is enough to drive anyone out of their home, Jane thought, hurrying over to her summerhouse, the alarm in her hands. She left it leaning against the inside wall and left the summerhouse door propped open. She wasn't worried about someone hearing the alarm and calling the police. Charity and Johnny knew what was going on, and the family next to them were on holiday. Her other neighbour was a field of sugar beet.

She decided to have an afternoon away from her private detective work to clear her head. She knew how she'd take her mind off things – she'd sew some marigold seeds for the summer – an African variety, whose packet promised ball-like yellow blooms, and some orange French marigolds. The two varieties should complement each other nicely, she thought, on her way to the greenhouse, the smoke alarm still ringing off and on behind her. To block out the noise she closed the greenhouse door.

Jane didn't care what others thought about marigolds. She had always liked them, finding them an attractive feature of any summer garden. Using an old trick she'd learnt years ago, she put a layer of used tea bags along the bottom of two propagator tubs, covered these with soil into which she dropped the seeds, gently pressing the soil down over them, and covered that with the layer of gravel. She wrote labels for both tubs, knowing she wouldn't be able to remember which was which once she'd stepped out of the greenhouse. This done, she went outside to fill a watering can from the tap in her back garden. She could still hear the alarm ringing off and on. It had now been ringing for some time. The mouse must have left by now, surely, she thought. Nothing could stand that much noise for that length of time could it? She looked over to the summerhouse, but couldn't see anything out of the ordinary. She didn't know what she'd expected to see – legions of mice streaming down its steps, maybe? She returned to her greenhouse, watering can in hand, having decided to leave the alarm ringing until its batteries went completely flat.

She left the tubs standing in water and went back to her cottage. She could still hear the alarm ringing, but much more faintly than before – its batteries almost spent. As she walked across the garden she thought about her conversation with Stella Barnes, mulling over what Stella had told her. One thing stuck in her mind – Johnny's father's love of motorbikes. He'd left on a motorcycle. He'd told Stella he'd wanted to open a motorcycle repair shop. Johnny himself was a keen motorcyclist. It was possible his father still had an interest in bikes after all these years? A love of motorcycles wasn't something that men really lost, was it, she asked herself. If Johnny's father was still a keen motorcyclist, maybe he went to motorbike rallies? There was bound to be one nearby sooner or later. It might be worth her while going to one and wandering around. Who knows? She might recognise him from his photograph alone, or someone else there might.

She was half way down her garden when a police car drew up alongside her house. A police officer got out off the car and walked over to her.

"Are you the house owner?" he asked her.

"I am," Jane replied, drying her hands on her jeans.

"We've had a report of an alarm ringing in your house. Someone walking across the field heard it and called us. They were worried you were being burgled."

"It's just the smoke alarm in my greenhouse," Jane explained. "I am trying to get rid of ..." she stopped. Did she really want the police to know she'd been trying to drive a wild mouse away? She didn't. "I left it out to change the batteries, but got involved with other things. I do apologise if you've been put to any trouble."

"You're trying to get rid of what?" the police officer asked her.

"Some insects overwintering in my greenhouse. I was trying to persuade them to leave and forgot all about the smoke alarm."

"Well as long as you're okay, love," he said.

"I most certainly am," she said, even though she was beginning to doubt her own mental state. She turned around to see Johnny staring out over the fence – with the corner of his collar in his mouth to indicate embarrassment and remorse. The police officer bid her goodbye and turned to leave, before stopping briefly to remind her how important it was that batteries in smoke alarms be changed regularly, adding, "My missus swears by rosewater as an insecticide. Gets rid of nasties without killing them."

"I'll try and remember that," Jane said. She looked over to her backdoor. Her Estonian home help, Maria, had arrived.

In her younger days, Jane did all her own housework. She'd enjoyed it, finding it cathartic and deriving pride on a job well done. But nowadays her sciatica made it less enjoyable and the demands her new job put on her, left her without enough time to do it as well as she'd like, and so she now employed Maria.

"Are you all right?" Maria asked, in her clipped Estonian accent, hurrying over to Jane, just as the police officer took his leave.

Jane explained what had just happened.

"You left alarm ringing to get rid of little mouse!" Maria said, looking at her as though Jane was touched. Jane realised how absurd it sounded.

"In Estonia we have a tried and tested way to get rid of mouse. We hit over head with heavy object!" Maria said, escorting Jane over to the summerhouse.

"But that would kill it."

"That's why we do," Maria said.

Maria picked up some of the hair from the summerhouse's floor, looking confused.

"It's for the mouse," Jane explained limply, removing the batteries from the smoke alarm, which instantly fell silent.

"For its nest?" Maria asked.

"It's meant to help drive it away. Hopefully it will have gone by now."

"If I see, I dispose," Maria said, with a glint in her eye.

"Please don't tell me how you dispose if you do," Jane said, leaving Maria sweeping up the hair from the floor.

When she closed the door behind her, she could swear she heard Maria mutter, "I don't know. Sometimes very clever lady. Other times stupid old woman."

She returned to the house, still thinking about motorbike rallies. She knew the best person to accompany her to a motorbike rally was Johnny Lambert, but as she couldn't ask him, she'd ask the next best person instead – her near neighbour – Felix Dawson-Jones, the husband of her good friend Mirabella Dawson-Jones, the rector of Failsham. Felix had been a keen motorcyclist when a young man by all accounts. She telephoned him. He needed little persuasion.

"I've been wanting to buy myself a Harley for years, but Mirabella won't let me. Something about my reflexes not being what they used to be and the weight I carry," he confided with a sigh. "But thanks to you, I now have an excuse to hire one for the day!" he said gleefully.

CHAPTER FIFTEEN

The Fig Leaf

I

On the other side of Failsham, Johnny, still a long way short of
the money he needed to take Charity skiing, was back by the
roadside again, complete with sandwich board. This time, he
didn't have to wait long for a car to pull up alongside.

"I drove past you the other day. Seeing you with your sandwich board gave me an idea. I asked my other half to do it, but
he refused," the female driver said.

"Refused to do what?" Johnny asked suspiciously.

"Walk around Failsham handing out flyers advertising our
new wine bar – the Fig Leaf…" the girl said. Johnny knew
there had to be a catch. "…wearing this!" she added, removing
a rug to reveal a sandwich board lying across the back seat of
her car. Johnny stared at it.

"You're kidding," he said.

"I've got a thong you could wear under it."

"You want me to walk around Failsham, wearing nothing
but a thong under a sandwich board with a Fig Leaf painted on
it! In March?"

"Clothes will ruin the effect. Could be worse, we could've opened a place called the Frankfurter," she quipped.

"Very droll."

As Johnny hesitated, she said: "Seventy pounds for a few hours work – cash."

"One hundred."

"Only if you flirt."

"What's your name? You're very pretty."

"Not with me – with the punters. Get lots of pretty girls in, and the men will follow. Basic rules of the hospitality business."

II

Johnny studied himself in a shop window. For a man wearing a knee length sandwich board with a Fig Leaf painted on both sides of it, a thong, a pair of open-toed sandals and a garland of gold ivy, he didn't think he looked that bad. He rubbed his goose pimpled arms. He'd been warmer in the broiler unit, but not as well paid. He spotted a table of young women smoking outside a coffee bar. He walked over to them and handed out some flyers.

"It's a new wine bar opening at the weekend. Show this at the bar and you get ten percent off a bottle of wine."

"Do we get to see what's underneath the sandwich board if we turn up?" one of the girls asked.

"Cheeky," Johnny said. "What about you, love?" he asked a young woman sitting by herself at another table. "You like a flyer?"

"I'll take all of them," she said.

"Don't push it – one only. You have to pay to drink the place dry."

III

Two and a half hours into his shift, Johnny stopped outside the gents. He realised he could only get in by squeezing in sideways or taking his sandwich board off. He chose the latter, leaving it and the gold garland in the alleyway outside.

When he returned the sandwich board had gone and the garland lay scattered in pieces, as though it had been kicked against the wall a few times. Johnny looked up and down the alleyway, but there was no sign of anyone. Reluctantly he emerged from the alleyway into the main thoroughfare, wearing only a thong and the sandals. There was no sign of the sandwich board. A few people stopped to stare at him. Johnny dived into a nearby shop.

"I don't suppose you've seen anyone with the sandwich board I was wearing?" he asked the shopkeeper. "Someone's nicked it." The shopkeeper solemnly shook his head whilst his assistant collapsed with laughter.

"Tea towel?" the shopkeeper offered.

IV

Johnny called Charity from the wine bar half an hour later. "The owner was none too pleased when I got back without her board, poor girl!"

"She still pay you?" Charity asked.

"Of course. For my troubles I got a hundred pounds in cash and a nice big slice of apple pie someone had baked her as a good luck present, so I'm happy. Tell you something, though," he added. "Women are like animals when they see a drop-dead gorgeous, half-naked, virile young man running through the streets with nothing but a tea towel wrapped around him. Had I known this earlier, I wouldn't have bothered buying all those clothes!"

"Ha! Ha!"

Johnny started to trudge home, his own sandwich board under his arm. A car drew up beside him, and the driver wound down the window.

"Can you sing?" the motorist asked.

Johnny stared at him. The motorist pointed at Johnny's plea for work sandwich board. "Can you sing?" he repeated.

"And dance," Johnny replied, summoning enough strength to dance a quick jig.

"I want someone to serenade my girlfriend for me," the motorist explained. "Can't do it myself, I'm tone deaf."

"By moonlight?" Johnny asked jokingly.

"When else?" was the reply. "Her name is Emma Greenlee."

CHAPTER SIXTEEN

Hell's Angels?

As was her custom whenever she visited the Rectory, Jane stopped off at the churchyard where Hugh was buried to visit his grave. She was upset to find an empty can on it. She removed it, and the flowers she'd left there few days earlier. These she replaced with a fresh display. She noticed a tiny piece of moss growing on Hugh's gravestone and picked it off with her fingernails. As she stood up, she saw Felix Dawson-Jones walking towards her, wearing leathers (suitable enough attire as they were off to a bikers' rally) and carrying a large cardboard box.

"Not more rubbish," Felix said of the can in Jane's hand. "Don't people know what a bin is? Put it in here," he instructed, shaking the cardboard box. She dropped the can into it. "I've spent the last hour clearing up the rubbish left here from the night before! Look at this lot," he said, holding out the box. As well as some empty wine bottles and cigarette packets, there was a broken china elephant and the top of a child's bubble-blowing kit lying in the box. "Sometimes I wonder what people think churchyards are actually for? Mirabella's going to write a blog for the church's website about the kind of things people leave behind in graveyards. We could open a Lost and Found, you know!"

Felix continued his rant while they walked through the churchyard towards the Rectory. "We've found bags, books, jackets, shoes, fur coats, handwritten manuscripts, and I don't know how many candles. I couldn't tell you the amount of candles I've found in churchyards in my time! Candles and churchyards go together like horses and carriages. The other day I found a pair of false teeth, and not for the first time. You'd think their owner would notice they weren't in! I even found one half of a twenty pound note, someone had ripped in half. Unfortunately I couldn't find the other half. Trust me, I looked!"

Jane glanced in the box. There was indeed a candle in it. But no false teeth.

When they reached the Rectory, Felix deposited the box full of rubbish on its steps, while Jane walked over to the motorbike parked on its front drive.

"I borrowed it from my cousin," Felix explained. "He's another keen motorcyclist. It's a Triumph Daytona 675 – the ultimate sports bike." Felix sounded as excited as a child.

Jane was just glad to see it had the sidecar she'd requested. The tragic death of her dear sister had left her with a terror of riding pillion. There was also her age and sciatica to consider. The rally was two hours drive away. As she climbed into the sidecar, Jane caught sight of Mirabella watching them from the front window, giving a slightly disapproving shake of her head. Jane waved as she and Felix set off for the rally, with him behind the Triumph's wheel and she at his side.

Jane and Felix had both believed their bike would be the only one there with a sidecar, but when they swept through the rally gates, a motorbike with a sidecar was on their tail. They parked at the end of the row of bikes with sidecars, as the motorbike behind them pulled up next to them. Its owners nodded to Jane and Felix, who nodded back. Jane climbed out of the sidecar, assisted by Felix. She was rather stiff and needed to bend her knees a few times to loosen up.

She looked around. While many there were large, leather clad middle-aged men with beards, there were also quite a few women at the rally and children. Whilst neither Jane nor Felix could be said to be the youngest there, neither were they the oldest. The bike park was almost full. Motorbikes of every make and vintage were parked there, many as covered in images of snakes, mermaids, pirates, skeletons, and naked women as their owners were. Felix and Jane followed the crowd in the general direction of the rally, the noise of motorcycles and live music grew louder and louder as they approached and the smell of food, grease and tire-rubber grew stronger. Jane stopped to admire a giant fake snake wrapped around the frame of a bike, its head across the handlebars, only to shudder and hurry away when she realised the snake wasn't foam, but stuffed.

Once through the ticket gate, the two bought beers. Clutching a pint of beer in one hand, and a print of the photograph of Johnny's father in the other, Jane and Felix strolled around the rally, hoping to catch sight of Pete Lambert.

They stopped outside the central arena. The sound of screaming spectators, stamping feet and roaring bikes coming from inside the arena was nothing compared to the noise thrown off from the row of competitively revving motorcyclists waiting to enter it. The noise was almost deafening. Most of the men still had their visors up allowing Jane to look along the row. Of those whose faces she could see, none were the man she was looking for. A hooter went off causing Jane to jump and the bikes to roar into the arena, one after the other, each attempting a wheelie as it entered. When the last of the motorcycles was through the gates they slammed shut.

They walked to some nearby stalls where Felix tried on a leather jacket. "Me?" he asked, giving a little twirl, his arms outstretched to show off the back of the jacket where, in red stitching, something half (naked) female and half-dragon was emblazoned.

"Definitely," Jane said.

Felix returned the jacket to its rail and they carried on.

They stopped by a stall offering bike repairs, where two men squatted by a Suzuki, deep in conversation. "Here's your enemy," one of the men said, holding a tiny sweet paper in his hand. "It was in the petrol tank!"

The bike owner almost kicked his own bike over. "No wonder it kept stalling!" he said, before swearing a number of times in quick succession. "Who would want to do that to me? What harm have I ever done anyone?" he wailed, close to tears.

"It's the old green-eyed monster, mate," his friend assured him. "It makes people go stir crazy, look what happened to old Kenny!"

They walked on, all the while scanning the crowd. Felix pointed to a clairvoyant's tent. Before Jane could stop him, he'd disappeared inside it, with the words, "She may be able to help."

Jane followed him. For the price of a pint of beer, Jane was allowed to choose a stick containing her fortune, from a pot containing many similar sticks. From inside the stick selected, she pulled out her fortune and read it out loud, "It says: 'Join the dots!'" Jane looked at the clairvoyant. "No suggestions as to how?"

The clairvoyant smiled enigmatically, while Felix shrugged.

From there they joined a crowd watching a band on stage. "I don't know about you, but I've seen quite a few people who could be Johnny's father. Like that guy over there." Felix nodded towards a man facing the stage, who was clapping along with the band. "I'll give it a shot." He walked over to the man and tapped him once on the shoulder. "Peter, is it you?" he asked. When the man looked blank, Felix said, "Sorry, I thought you were someone else." Felix patted him on the shoulder and returned to Jane.

"It was worth a shot," she said.

The two continued to walk around the rally. Now and then, one or other would approach a man about the same age as Johnny's father and ask if he were 'Peter?' They had to stop when someone said, ".You've asked me that already? What the hell's wrong with you? You fancy me or something!"

Felix returned quickly to Jane, saying, "I think we're going to have to try something else."

Jane stared away in the distance, wondering what they could do. She watched as some men raced their motorbikes around a makeshift track, weaving in and around haystacks. After a while she gave click of her fingers, which Felix immediately mimicked.

"I know what we can do!" she said.

With Felix buying them both a sandwich, Jane went to speak to the young man at the ticket kiosk: "I'm trying to find a friend of mine. We arranged to meet here, but I think he must have forgotten. His name is Pete Lambert."

"Could Pete Lambert come to the ticket sales at the North entrance, where his friend Jane is waiting to kick his ass for forgetting to meet her there," the tannoy announced. While Jane appreciated the gesture, she couldn't help wondering whether anybody could hear the tannoy over the din.

A few minutes later the same announcement was repeated. This did the trick. Within minutes, two men arrived at the kiosk both claiming to be Pete Lambert. The two arrived from different directions. The young man in the kiosk pointed in the direction of Jane.

The first man to wander over to Jane was far too young to be Johnny's father. He had an irate looking girlfriend with him, who visibly calmed down when she saw the Jane who wanted to speak to her boyfriend.

"Different Pete Lambert, I think," she said.

"'fraid so," Jane said. "But thanks for taking the time."

As the young couple walked away, Jane heard him say, "See – I told you – I don't know anyone called Jane."

While the first Pete Lambert placated his girlfriend, the second walked over to Jane. He was about the right age.

"Well, as I don't know you, I can't be the Pete Lambert you're looking for either. How many of us are there out there?" he joked.

"Actually, you might be the man I'm looking for," Jane said. "May I have a few minutes of your time, now you're here?"

"I think I should warn you I'm taken, love," he said, pretending to back away, his hands mockingly raised in the air.

Jane took out the photograph of Johnny's father. Although the young man in the photograph didn't look much like the man standing in front of her, the photograph had been taken nearly thirty years earlier. She showed it to Pete Lambert. "This is a photograph taken many years ago of a man with the same name as yourself."

"And? What the hell is all this about? Who are you?"

"I'm not from the Police, nor the Inland Revenue, or the Child Support Agency or anything of the kind," Jane said hurriedly. "I'm just trying to help a near neighbour of mine to find his father."

"I don't know who you are, or what this is about, lady," Pete Lambert said angrily. "Even if I was your neighbour's father – which I'm not – I wouldn't tell you. If I'd walked out, then I didn't want to be there, did I? If I knew the man in that photograph, which I don't, I wouldn't tell you. We mind our own business here, got it?" he said, having by now, moved to stand extremely close to Jane.

She'd got it, but in case she hadn't the young man at the ticket kiosk joined them. Not only that, but she couldn't help noticing an angry-looking group of men advancing on her. Out of the corner of her eye she saw Felix appear, look alarmed, drop the sandwiches he was carrying and run over to her.

"I think you'd better leave," the ticket seller said.

"Yeah! Clear off!" someone else said, even though he'd just joined the throng, and couldn't have any idea what the argument was about. Jane thought it unlikely the group would beat up a woman of her age, but she didn't want to give them any excuses.

"We'll leave immediately," she said. "I'm sorry if I made you angry. I was trying to help a good friend find his father. A father he hasn't seen since he was a child. A man, who for all we know, might want to see his son again." She turned to Pete Lambert and said, "I'm sorry you're not my friend's father."

Jane and Felix walked away from the crowd as calmly as they could. Although they tried not to show it, they were both shaking and their pulses racing.

"Hold on," Pete Lambert shouted after them. They both stopped. They glanced nervously at each other, and turned around to face him. "Let's have a look at that photo. One of us might know him."

The group of men handed the photograph around in turn. Each stared at it, only to shake their heads. "No, don't know him." "Sorry, can't help." "Any of you lot seen him?" someone asked. Unfortunately no one in the group had. Eventually the photograph was returned to Jane.

"There's a Lost and Found board in the beer tent," the kiosk man said. "You could pin your photograph up there. Someone might recognise him. I think someone's plugged a laptop in there. You could post details of him on our website."

CHAPTER SEVENTEEN

The Chase

On their way back to the beer tent, Felix stopped to pick up the two sandwiches he'd dropped moments earlier. He stared at them. Both were squashed flat. One had a footprint on it.

"That baying mob's trampled them underfoot," he said indignantly, throwing them in the bin.

"Better them than us," Jane replied.

The beer tent teemed with people, forcing Jane and Felix to stop immediately once through its entrance. Those in the tent weren't gathered around the bar but the tentpole. They clapped while a guitarist played snake-charming music. Jane and Felix both looked up. A man was attempting to climb to the top of the tent's central pole wearing only his underwear. The pole must have been twenty metres high. Jane looked away, fearing for the man's safety. Felix, however, joined the crowd and began to clap and chant: Higher! Higher!

Jane left him to it and walked around the tent until she found the Lost and Found board. She took some time to read it. The cork board was covered with notices and photographs. The left-hand side was taken up with missing biker paraphernalia, such as motorcycles, helmets, jackets, as well as the usual

Hammer Horror ads searching for missing body parts including, as Felix would put it, the obligatory false teeth. Were these the same ones Felix found in the churchyard, Jane wondered. Maybe she should put up a found notice to reunite teeth with toothless owner? She read the notice next to it. This featured a man grinning into the camera with a live rat sitting on his shoulders, holding the stuffed rodent equivalent of a butterfly collection. Above the photograph was a handwritten notice stating:

'Yorkshire biker reunited with former pets! Thanks to everyone involved in hunt.'

Lovely, Jane thought, realising for the first time how passé it had been of them to bury Adele's dead pet hamster in the garden, rather than stuffing and framing it.

The right-hand side of the notice board contained the missing people ads. These had mostly been placed by people trying to track down old friends or old flames. The most poignant ad there had been placed by the parents of a man missing since aged eighteen, last seen driving away from a motorcycle rally. He'd now be thirty-two, Jane realised, staring at a photograph of the young man, pinned next to their ad. Jane could only hope he was safe and well, wherever he was.

She removed a card announcing the safe return of a studded jacket to its owner, turned it over, and on its rear wrote:

'Missing! Last seen twenty-eight years ago, then called Pete(r) Mark Lambert. Pete, your son wants to get in touch. Interested? Please call...'

After adding her mobile phone number, she pinned her card up on the board, leaving enough room for the photograph to be pinned beside it. This she scanned onto the laptop before typing her message to Pete Lambert below it and posting it onto the rally's webpage. This done, she pinned the photograph on the notice board under her hand-written message.

She wasn't sure what more she could do and made her way back to the entrance. Just as she reached it, screaming broke out and the guitarist began playing the *Striptease*. Jane looked up to discover the man at the top of the tent pole had removed his underwear, which he waved around his head with one hand, while firmly gripping the tent pole with the other. Jane looked away; she was a respectable widow woman, after all.

She met up with Felix outside.

"Apparently that's his party trick. He goes around the tent afterwards collecting money in his Y-fronts. Any luck?" he asked her.

"I left a message. We'll have to see if it produces a response. Do you mind waiting a while longer just in case somebody telephones me?"

"On the contrary," Felix said, taking out a handkerchief with which he mopped his brow. "I can carry on re-living my youth and pretend it's all in the name of duty."

They returned to the main arena, just as a young mother left it, dragging a reluctant child with each hand behind her, "If we leave now, we'll miss the traffic," the young mother said.

"But I bought a ticket for the raffle!" one of the children said.

"Oh those things never win," her mother replied.

"Why did you tell me to use my pocket money to buy one then?" the child argued, angrily throwing something on the ground behind her.

Once the family had passed them, Felix picked it up. It was a scrunched up raffle ticket, on the back of which was written Wardrobe. With the family no longer in view, Felix popped the ticket into his pocket, before following Jane inside.

He sat down beside her, about halfway along the back row, and settled down to watch a race between twenty motorcyclists.

"He who comes last comes first!" a voice over the loudhailer informed the audience. "Coming first's for losers!"

A hooter signalled the start of the race. Each motorcyclist drove as slowly as he or she could manage. One by one, the contestants either fell off their bikes or their bikes stalled. By the end of the first lap sixteen had come off their bikes. Two more quickly followed, leaving only two. As each contestant jumped off their bike, they removed their helmets, allowing Jane to scrutinise them. All the male contestants were too young to be Johnny's father. One might be a half-brother, she thought, but then so might half the rally.

Down on the sand track, the two surviving race contestants slowed down even further, whereupon one immediately fell off. This left the rider of a silver-blue Toyota the winner. To rapturous applause from the audience, he gave a victory lap, arm held aloft. Jane and Felix got to their feet to join the audience in a standing ovation. Jane glanced at the phone in her hand, but it remained silent. She decided to buy them both a coffee.

By the time she got back, another contest was underway in the arena below. Bikes lined up next to each other, roped to heavy objects: a sledge weighed down with bricks; a wardrobe; a fridge freezer; a large stone statue, and at the end of the row, a wheel-less caravan. While the bikes warmed up, rally staff placed tombolas with the names of the various objects on them, along the track.

"Ah!" Felix said, patting the raffle ticket in his pocket.

Within a few minutes of the hooter sounding, the rope attached to the caravan had snapped, bricks from the sledge littered the track, the arms had fallen off the statue, and the fridge freezer was in pieces, leaving Wardrobe with a clear run to the end.

"Let's make it a bit harder for him!" a voice said over the loudspeaker, as other motorcyclists hurriedly attached their bikes to the caravan, and gave chase. Some in the audience cheered, others booed.

Wardrobe glanced over his shoulder and tried to go faster, but his load made that impossible. The others may have been dragging a wheel-less caravan around the track, but there were many more of them and they were catching him up. The audience, including Felix, jumped to their feet.

"Wardrobe!" "Wardrobe!" "Caravan!" "Caravan!" they shouted.

"Come on you Wardrobe!" Felix yelled.

Jane took the opportunity to remove some theatre binoculars from her bag with which to study the crowd again. Most people were too focused on the action to notice. Her search was fruitless. No one she saw reminded her enough of either Johnny, or the photograph of his father, to make it worth her while approaching them.

In the arena below, it was neck to neck in the sprint to the winning line. Caravan had lost one and a half sides, its back door hung open and most of its furniture now covered the track. Wardrobe wasn't in much better condition. After a concerted effort, Team Caravan crossed the winning line first, whereupon the caravan's remaining side fell off and it rolled over.

Wardrobe leapt off his bike, pointed to the other contestants and raised six fingers in the air then he pointed to himself and raised one finger in the air.

"Fair?" he yelled.

Over the loudspeaker a voice said, "No one said we were playing by the Marquis of Queensberry's rules! I formally declare Caravan the winner. We will now spin the tombola containing the tickets bought by all you clever people who correctly predicted Caravan would ultimately triumph."

A raffle ticket was pulled from the tombola labelled Caravan and held aloft to the crowd. "The proud winner of a keg of beer is blue seventy-eight! Blue seventy-eight! A worthy winner!"

A woman from the audience made her way into the arena to fetch her prize.

"Boo!" people shouted. "Cheat!" "Hiss!" "Should have been Wardrobe!"

Felix jumped to his feet, waved his raffle ticket in the air, and joined in the crowd shouting, "We was robbed!"

"Okay! Okay!" the referee said over the loudspeaker. A young member of staff spun the tombola drum marked Wardrobe and pulled a raffle ticket from it. "A second keg of beer goes to pink one hundred and three! Pink one hundred and three!"

Felix stared at the ticket in his hand. It was white twenty-five. He sat down.

Entertaining though this was, Jane was growing annoyed. She still hadn't seen any face in the crowd which reminded her of Johnny, or the photograph of his father, nor had anyone responded to her message. She checked the time. They'd been there for most of the day and still had to get home. "I think we may have to leave it and hope someone gets in touch, Felix," she said.

"Whatever you want to do, Jane."

They got to their feet and made their way to the end of their row. They waited to join the crowds pushing their way up the stairwell, when a man walking past them on his way towards the exit, inadvertently dropped a photograph. Felix stared at it, but before he could say anything, the man picked it up, and moved on.

"That was your photograph!" Felix said.

"Are you sure?" Jane asked.

"Quite sure."

Jane stared at the man. He was middle aged, quite tall, as was Johnny, and balding. He was clad in leather and he held a motorbike helmet under his arm, and more importantly, he was about to leave the arena.

"I never thought I'd hear myself say this, but follow that biker!" Jane said.

The two hurried after him, following him into the bike park. He was parked some way from their bike, but they were closer to the entrance than he. When they got to their bike they were both a bit breathless, but they couldn't afford to dawdle. The man concerned already sat astride his bike, putting on his helmet. Soon he'd start his bike and join the queue waiting to exit the rally. Jane quickly climbed into the sidecar, while Felix jumped onto their bike and prepared for the chase.

Minutes later they roared down the motorway, after the biker. Jane did not feel at all easy. In order not to lose their man, Felix had to drive extremely quickly and weave in and out of the traffic, throwing Jane from one side of the side-car to the other, despite her seatbelt. To steady herself, she held onto the sides with both hands. Her sciatica was beginning to play up, but when she tried to ask Felix to slow down, a fly flew into her mouth. She couldn't even take her hands from the side to remove it. Eventually she spat it out, but the side car wasn't covered and she was hit in the face with her own spittle. After wiping her face, she said, as loudly as she could, "Felix, I think we're travelling too quickly."

Felix couldn't have heard her because instead of slowing down, he speeded up, shouting, 'Woo Ha!' at the top of his voice.

Well I'm glad you're enjoying the thrill of the chase, Felix Dawson-Jones, she, who couldn't remember the last time she had been so uncomfortable, thought. This chase reminded Jane of her pursuit of another Peter only the month before. Another Peter who enjoyed racing up and down motorways, and another one with a morally ambiguous character.

To Jane's enormous relief, the motorcyclist pulled in at a petrol station just up ahead of them to fill up. Felix followed him, pulling into the other side of the pump used by the motorcyclist. Jane decided to wait for the motorcyclist in the garage shop. He appeared minutes later. She allowed him to pay for his petrol, before approaching him with the words: "Pete Lambert?"

"Who love?" he replied.

"Pete Lambert. That's the name of the man in the photograph you took from the Lost and Found board at the rally. I know you have it. I saw you drop it and pick it up again. I put the photograph on the board, you see. Do you still use the name Pete Lambert, or do you go by another name?"

"Ah," he said, sheepishly. "Got me!"

Now she could study him more closely, she couldn't see any resemblance in him to Johnny. He was also too young to be Johnny's father. She did not think she had her man.

"Before you go on I need to tell you something," the man in front of her said. "I'm not the man in the photograph. I don't know who he is. For a start I'm only forty-two, and he's going to be a lot older than that now, let's face it."

"Why did you take the photograph?"

"My daughter likes to collect old fashioned photographs for her school folder. The guy's hair and his clothes, well they're dated by our standards. She loves stuff like that. I didn't think anyone would notice. Sorry," he said, handing her the photograph. He gave her an embarrassed shrug before he left the shop.

She walked over to Felix, who waited to pay for the petrol. He'd heard everything.

"I'll wait for you outside," Jane said wearily.

She was upset more than anything. Felix joined her minutes later. He'd bought her a bag of fruit and nuts. She opened and began to eat them.

"Do you want to go back to the rally?" he asked.

She shook her head. "No. He wasn't there. Or he didn't want to be found. Let's go home."

When they reached the bike, Felix gave a little holler of delight. He'd found a small blue envelope inside the crisps he'd bought himself, promising a cash prize or some free crisps. He opened it, grinned, and showed it to Jane. The envelope contained nothing more than a picture of a man spread-eagled against a brick wall, and the words: 'Better luck next time!'

"I know just how he feels," Jane said. She threw the bag of nuts into the bin. "They're stale. Like the trail to Johnny's father!"

CHAPTER EIGHTEEN

There's Only One Emma Greenlee

I

The property where Emma Greenlee and her flatmate lived was part of a terrace of newly built houses constructed from pale yellow brickwork, forming one side of a square, which overlooked a communal lawned garden. Each house had a small upper-floor balcony, just large enough for one person to stand on.

At just after ten o'clock Johnny, flanked by Charity and Jack, arrived in the square. Emma's boyfriend, Kevin, walked over to join them.

"That's her house, the one in the middle," Kevin said, pointing at the house in question. They all looked over to it. "She has the bedroom at the front. She always goes to bed at ten-fifteen. Now, as I'm meant to be doing the serenading, not you, would you mind serenading her from under the balcony, where she can't see you?"

Johnny did as he was instructed. While he positioned himself directly underneath Emma's balcony, her boyfriend strode across the lawn. About halfway across, he turned around to face Emma's house. Charity and Jack stayed where they were.

On the dot of ten-fifteen, the light went on in Emma's bedroom; her boyfriend raised his arm. This was the cue for Johnny to begin singing. To the tune of *O Sole Mio* by Di Capua, he sang:

"There's just one Emma Greenlee. Will you appear?

Oh Emma Greenlee – appear to me-e-e."

As Johnny belted the first verse out, Kevin mimed the words, complete with arm movements and facial expressions. People crossing the square stopped to watch. Some opened their windows and put their heads outside. A few even left their houses to gather in the gardens, and by the time Emma appeared on her balcony, there was quite a crowd of onlookers. Emma looked both embarrassed and flattered. Charity nudged Jack. It was going well.

Meanwhile Johnny continued singing, and Kevin miming.

"Oh Emma Greenlee,

From Stoke on Trently,

I so love you,

Will you marry me-e-e?"

Kevin through his arms out expansively, tilted his head back, and opened his mouth as wide as he could. On the words: 'Will you marry me?' he knelt on the ground, hands clasped as though in prayer.

Johnny was just about to repeat the verse, when he heard a voice above him ask, "Excuse me, but who are you?"

He looked up. In his enthusiasm, he'd inadvertently stepped out from under the balcony and into view. Emma continued to peer down at him. Johnny glanced in her boyfriend's direction. So did Emma.

"Emm!" Kevin said, running towards her. "I can't hit a note – you know that – so I hired someone to do it for me. But I wrote the words!"

"He did," Johnny said.

"From the heart," Kevin said.

"I don't know what to say," Emma said.

Kevin stopped running, knelt down beneath her balcony, and said, "Emma Greenlee, will you marry me?"

Emma looked at the crowd then back to her boyfriend, before raising her arms above her head and shouting at the top of her voice: "Yes!"

The crowd cheered and clapped. Emma's front door was opened by her crying flatmate, while Emma jumped up and down, shouting, "I'm engaged! I'm engaged!"

Johnny, rather concerned that the balcony wasn't designed for someone to jump up and down on it, ran over to Emma's boyfriend and shook his hand vigorously. "Congratulations mate," he said.

A quick glance at the balcony showed both men that Emma had gone indoors.

"Thanks," her boyfriend mumbled, pressing the thirty pounds promised into Johnny's hand. He disappeared through the open front door, only to reappear almost immediately. He took out another twenty pounds which he also pressed into Johnny's hands with the words, "She said yes!" This time he hugged Johnny before disappearing indoors again only to reappear for the second time.

"If you still need work, Emma's granddad's looking for someone to help him lay a patio out front. He's in his seventies and needs a bit of a hand. I can dig his number out for you, if you want?"

II

"He seems a nice enough old boy," Johnny said on the way home, after coming off the phone to Emma's grandfather. "He just wants someone to help him with the heavy lifting. The front gardens of those bungalows on Boland Close aren't very big. If I get round for nine tomorrow morning, I reckon I'll be home by lunchtime."

"You really don't have to keep doing this, you know?" Charity said.

"Yes I do," Johnny said, "I'm going to prove to you two that I'm no longer the feckless, useless, son-of-a-bitch you fell in love with."

"What if we like the other guy better?" Jack asked.

Johnny put his arms around Charity and Jack. "You won't," he promised.

CHAPTER NINETEEN

Monty

I

Jane's business mobile rang. The caller's number was withheld, but she answered it even so.

"Jane Hetherington speaking."

"Yeah my name's Monty. I'm calling about that message on the rally's website. About the man whose son is looking for him..." a male voice said "... Pete Lambert."

"Do you have any information about his whereabouts?" Jane said, her heart almost missing a beat.

"I think so. I used to work at a bus depot with someone who looked just like the man in the photo. He was called Pete Lambert. He had a son he didn't see. Can't remember all the details, didn't know him that well really, but he'd be about the right age."

"Do you have any idea where he might be now?"

"Not any more. Don't work there no more. He left before me. Heard he'd moved to Hull. I could ask around like. I'm still in touch with a few people from the depot, plus I got mates in

Hull. They might know where he is. Thought I'd be speaking to Pete's son as a matter of fact. You the mother?"

"No, I'm a friend of his. I'm acting as an intermediary. How long ago did you work with Pete Lambert?"

"Oh now let me see. Seven or eight years ago, something like that. Like I said, I didn't know him that well, but I remember him mentioning he had a son he never saw. I'd never do that, me. If I had a kid, I'd make sure I was part of his life."

"I don't suppose he left a forwarding address?"

"Guess not. I could try and find out more."

"You're being very helpful," Jane said, wondering if she was about to be asked for money.

Monty must have read her mind because he said, "You probably think I'm just some bullshiter on the make!"

Jane was about to say, of course I don't, when Monty said, "I've got a group photo with me and him in it. Someone took a picture of everyone at the depot and I asked for a copy. I'm happy to show it to you, to prove I'm legit."

"In that case we should meet up," Jane said.

Before the call ended, they'd arranged a place and time to meet.

Call over, Jane was left to reflect. She was pleased by the turn of events, although whether this would turn into something remained to be seen. While her caller had been short on facts, nothing he'd told her flatly contradicted the possibility that he had actually worked with Johnny's father. What's more, he had a photo. Maybe, finally, she was closing in on her prey. She did hope so. The fruitless search for Johnny's father was proving frustrating and upsetting. It was all very well being a private detective who prided herself on her efficiency, but what

116

was the point, if she couldn't even help her closest friends? She was dragged from her thoughts by the arrival of the post.

She found a letter waiting for her on her doorstep. She recognised the handwriting. She opened it. It contained a poem, although not for her. It was addressed to the mouse in the summerhouse.

> **To the mouse in the summerhouse**
> *'Rather than peeve us, it's time to leave us.*
> *We all like guests, but you're a pest.*
> *Don't play dumb, it's wearisome.*
> *Save us the rigmarole, find a new watering hole.*
> *Please don't tease, just pack up your cheese,*
> *and be on your way, eater of hay.'*
> See you tonight, Jane - Your Stanman'

II

Although Jane couldn't entertain the thought of entering into a relationship with another man, not just yet anyway, there were men in her life to whom she was close. There was Johnny next door, for example, and Jack, although he was really more a surrogate grandson than anything else. Then there was Felix Dawson-Jones and Ant Dillard, the chair of the Magistrate's Court where Jane was a part-time Magistrate. He was more than a colleague, he was a good friend.

There was also Stanley Marshman, a well-known writer of comic poetry, which he published under the nickname by which Jane had always known him – Stanman. Jane had once been in love with Stan, and had even become engaged to him.

She was just eighteen at the time, and he only slightly older. That teenage relationship had been about sex and a misguided teenage belief that young lovers always lived happily ever after. They hadn't. Jane had married Hugh, and Stan a girl called Elsie. Thereafter their lives had diverged.

It had been Jane who'd contacted Stan after Hugh's death. She hadn't thought long and hard about it. It was something she did, just like when she became a private detective. It felt right and so she did it. They'd met up. Elsie was still alive, she learnt, but in the grip of dementia, the woman she'd once been, lost to her family forever.

At that first reunion, both agreed that whilst neither was ready for the type of relationship they had once enjoyed, neither wished to lose touch again for decades as they had before. Their monthly evening get-togethers, such as the one they'd arranged for that very evening, were to ensure they didn't. She smiled to herself. She was looking forward to her evening out.

III

The poem reminded her to check her summerhouse to ensure the hair and the siren had driven the mouse away permanently. One look inside told her they hadn't. She returned with a dust-pan and brush.

"How am I going to get rid of you, my friend?" she said to her rodent lodger while she swept the summerhouse floor.

This was like the time the ants invaded her kitchen her first summer in the Pink Cottage. Jane, still young and naive, hadn't wanted to use chemicals, unlike her husband. She'd visited the library to research alternative, natural ant-deterrent, returning with a list.

"They have a very sophisticated sense of smell," she'd explained, pouring scented talcum powder over the back doorstep. "If this doesn't work, something else on the list will," she'd added.

"If you say so, dear," Hugh had replied.

The talcum powder wasn't much of a deterrent, any more than was the salt, vinegar, baking soda, peppermint oil, black pepper, nor even a noxious mixture of all of them, which she'd spread over the back doorstep in desperation.

The attempt to rid her property of the ants humanely had ended with her looking down on the ants swarming across her so-called deterrent, under her back door and into her kitchen, and Hugh looking at her.

"Okay," she'd said, thrusting a carton of ant powder into his hand, "you win."

She looked around her summerhouse one last time and sighed. Before she left, she pinned Stan's poem on the wall. It would give the mouse something to read if nothing else.

She returned to her cottage to find Charity waiting by her back door.

"That mouse is back," Jane said.

"A nice blow dry and set will take your mind off it," Charity replied, following her into the house.

They moved to the bathroom, where Jane took her normal place in front of the mirror, with Charity behind her, hairdressing equipment laid out at her side. "I think I'll put some colour through, Jane, to lighten it. It's nearly spring after all, and..."

"And?"

"I know – you and Stan are just good friends, but you still want to look your best for this evening, don't you?"

"I always want to look my best, Charity."

"Exactly!"

While Charity mixed up a thick orange paste in a bowl, she asked Jane how the search for Johnny's father was going.

"It's been like looking for a needle in a haystack, Charity. Everywhere I've looked, I've drawn a blank. Even Stella was unable to shed any light on things. However, I think I've got a new lead though – someone who says he used to work with a Pete Lambert. He thinks it might be the same Pete Lambert who is Johnny's father. He says he's even got a photograph to prove it. We're going to meet up. Hopefully it will lead to something."

"And what if it does? We don't even know if his dad will want to meet him. He hasn't made much attempt to get in touch so far, has he?" Charity said, applying the colour to Jane's hair. "Say you find him, and Johnny contacts him and he's not interested. Then what?"

"I hear what you're saying, Charity, but surely you don't want me to abandon my search without telling Johnny, do you?" Jane asked. She would have some reservations about this.

"I just don't want him getting kicked in the teeth again, that's all. He's been through enough."

"I don't want that either, Charity, you know that. But Johnny must have known what he was getting into when he asked me to help him find his missing father. I feel that unless he tells me otherwise, I must carry on."

"Say you found his dad. What's to stop you trying to find out if he wants Johnny back in his life before you say anything to him?"

"And if he doesn't?"

"Pretend you haven't been able to find him."

Jane wasn't sure about this. Charity may well be right. Johnny's father might well have no more interest in his son than he did when he abandoned him all those years ago. She didn't want Johnny to have the door slammed in his face by his father anymore than Charity did, nor did she want to have to tell Johnny that his father had rejected him for the second time. Charity's solution, a simple white lie — I have been unable to find your father, I'm sorry — would save his feelings, certainly, but might leave her feeling like a fraud. The truth might be crueller than the fiction, but the fiction would be a betrayal of his trust in her. Abandoning her search on the quiet was, in her view, no better. What to do?

"My goodness, Charity. What a can of worms we've opened," she said. "We'll just have to hope that if I am able to locate Johnny's father, he does want his son back in his life."

"And if he doesn't?"

"I think we'll have to cross that bridge, when we come to it. Where is Johnny, by the way?"

"Helping someone lay a patio."

CHAPTER TWENTY

Patio-Man

I

Johnny revised his first impression of Emma's granddad, when the 'nice enough old boy' opened the door with: "You're late!"

"No I'm not!" Johnny said, pointing to his watch. "You said nine o'clock. It's only nine now."

"I said to start at nine, which means you're late. You can start by digging up that lot and piling them up by the gate," Emma's grandfather said, pointing to the paving slabs, which covered two thirds of the small walled front garden. A flower-bed made up the rest of the garden. A spade leant up against the wall next to a wheelbarrow. "I'll be indoors eating my break-fast," the man said, shutting the door without another word.

The old Johnny would have walked away from the job there and then, but the new Johnny was determined to prove to his girlfriend that he could stick at things however tough those things got. Therefore he took his jacket off, rolled up his sleeves and got to work. Using the spade provided, he slowly loosened a paving slab and prised it up, walking it across the garden, to lean against the wall near to the gate. This done, he returned to the patio and removed the next paving slab.

By the time the front door opened again and patio-man, as Johnny had nicknamed him, stepped outside, Johnny had dug up and moved three of the seven rows of paving slabs.

"I've been watching you wasting time," patio-man snarled. "I'm not paying you money to spend all day texting."

"What?" Johnny replied, throwing his spade on the ground. He had no idea what patio-man was talking about. He pointed to his work, and was about to say, "Who do you think moved that lot?" when patio-man said, "I saw you on the phone."

Johnny suddenly realised patio-man must have overseen the brief text exchange he'd had with Charity over the purchase of milk. "I took two seconds to text the word okay to my girlfriend," Johnny said defensively.

"I'm not paying you good money to spend all day texting your girlfriend, and if you throw my spade on the ground again, you'll be buying me a new one! What are you standing around for now?" the man barked. "When you've finished moving the old ones, bring the new ones round from the back. I want that soil turned over and any roots and stones removed before you start laying the next lot. I'm going out for a paper, but my wife's inside and I've told her to keep an eye on you – so no more time wasting," he said menacingly, before leaving the garden.

Patio-man disappeared down the street, with Johnny staring after him indignantly, his hands on his waist, mouth open. Johnny knew if he left now, he wouldn't get paid for what he'd done, otherwise he'd be on his way home. What a nerve, Johnny thought to himself. He heard a loud rapping on the window and turned around to find his employer's wife pointing to the remaining paving slabs and mouthing the words, "Get working you!"

II

Patio-man returned hours later without the paper he'd left to buy, stopping by the gate to survey Johnny's work. New patio slabs covered one third of the garden, upturned soil the rest. Johnny, who felt quite proud of having managed to remove the old patio, and lay a third of its replacement in such a short time, waited expectantly for this to be remarked upon. It was.

"Haven't you finished yet?" patio-man said. There was a slur to his words and his breath stank of the beer.

Johnny stared coolly at patio-man for a few moments, before saying, "Oh, is there a pub nearby? I'll go and have my lunch then. See you later." He laid the spade against the wall, picked up his jacket, and walked down the road in the direction taken by patio-man.

He returned after lunch to find the patio as he'd left it, even the spade remained unmoved. The couple's car wasn't in the drive any more, he noticed, and the house stood in darkness. He knocked on the door a couple of times, to let them know he was back, but no one answered it.

"They've gone to her sisters," the couple's neighbour informed them, almost apologetically, through an opened downstairs window.

"They didn't happen to mention when they'd be back?"

"Won't be till late, if they get back tonight at all," the neighbour said, looking as though he felt rather sorry for Johnny.

Johnny knew what was going to happen. Whether he finished the job today or not, he was not going to get paid for it. Not for months anyway, and only then if he threatened legal action. Right, he thought. We'll see about that!

He looked at his watch. School would just be breaking up. He telephoned Jack. "I need you and as many of your friends as you can spare," he said.

It took Jack, and the two friends he bought with him, only a few minutes to arrive at the bungalow.

"You're going to put the old patio back?" Jack said.

"Every last paving slab. And I'm going to put the new ones back where I found them."

"Cool!" the boys all agreed.

With four pairs of hands on the job it didn't take Johnny and his team of helpers long to dig up the newly-laid patio slabs and replace them with the old ones. They returned the new slabs at the back of the house. Job complete, Johnny and his team surveyed their work.

"Good work, men. Fish and chips all round, I think," he said, just as a woman walked up to the property. She stopped and studied Johnny silently.

He would have put her in her mid-thirties. Johnny straightened himself up. Although it was only March, he was perspiring heavily, and had stripped off to the waist. He used his hand to mop his brow, and sweep his hair back. She looked him up and down. The boys looked at her and then back at Johnny.

"Found you at last," she said, "I've been looking everywhere for you."

III

Charity, Johnny and Jack, all arrived home at the same time.

"Johnny's going to be a glamour model," Jack announced the moment the three converged by the back door.

"You're going to be a what?" Charity asked.

"Some woman spotted me potential when she saw me streaking through Failsham in my thong, but she was in her car and couldn't stop. Said she's been looking for me for the last few days. She wants me to do some modelling for her on-line catalogue."

"Why you?" Charity asked suspiciously.

"What a ridiculous question. Because I'm young, handsome and way cheaper than a professional model, of course."

"What exactly does she want you to model?"

"Men's underwear."

"Basically he's going to take his kit off for money!" Jack said.

"Only ninety-nine percent of it," Johnny pointed out.

"You're going to do what?" Charity demanded, slamming the bag containing her hairdressing equipment down so hard on the ground that a couple of rollers fell out of it and rolled away.

"Keep your knickers on, old girl!" Johnny said, with a wink in Jack's direction.

"It's you keeping yours on, I'm worried about," she said.

"Charity! Please! It's not that type of catalogue, and I'm not that type of boy!"

CHAPTER TWENTY-ONE

Stan the Man

I

Jane and Stan met outside the Thai restaurant, where they were going to eat that night. It had started to rain only moments after Jane had set out for Southstoft, and it was still raining when she parked her car in a nearby car park. She walked to the restaurant protected by an umbrella. Stan was waiting for her.

"I hope you haven't been waiting long?" she said.

"No, no," he said, holding the door open for her. "Just arrived."

As the two were shown to their table, Jane thanked Stan for the poem. "I've pinned it to the summerhouse wall. He'll either get the message and leave, or stay and open a rodent poetry corner."

They were seated at a small corner table.

"May I compliment you on your outfit, Jane," Stan said of the black knee length cocktail dress Jane wore, over which she had swirled a deep red pashmina.

"Why thank you, Stan. It's so nice when a man actually notices when a woman makes an effort."

"My Elsie always used to hate it when I didn't say how nice she looked. 'I've taken hours over my appearance and you haven't even noticed,' she'd say. The rows we used to have about it." Suddenly he stopped talking and looked crestfallen, as he remembered the woman Elsie had once been.

"How are things at home, Stan?"

"She's deteriorating Jane. Without doubt. Sometimes she doesn't even recognise me any more," he said, fighting the tears back. "Take last night. I asked her to lay the table, like I always do. It's something for her to do – keeps things as normal as possible, even though it now takes her an hour when it used to take her ten minutes. Everything takes her so long nowadays. When I think how organised she used to be," he shook his head sadly. "I leave everything out. All she has to do is carry it from the sideboard to the table. Sometimes we have some fun and games – like the other day when I caught her putting a full glass of squash in the cabinet and asked her why. She said she was worried someone might knock it over if she left it on the table. It made me laugh. It was crazy, yet it sort of made sense. I just had to kiss her. It reminded me so much of the silly, kooky things she used to do all the time, but that's when she meant to," he said, lapsing into silence for a few moments. Jane knew he needed to talk about this. She said nothing, allowing him to recover. "Usually she can manage to lay a table. But yesterday I found her standing by the table with a plate in her hand. She didn't know what to do with it. She was completely lost. 'Nearly done?' I asked her. She stared straight through me. She didn't know who I was. I said, 'Elsie, it's me, Stan.' We've been married for more than forty years, but she didn't recognise me, Jane. We were both as terrified as each other. I took the plate from her and sat her down. Slowly she returned to me. What's left of her. Is this to be my life, Jane? Looking after someone who doesn't know who I am? I never thought this would happen."

"Nobody ever does. We all live our lives hoping the worst doesn't happen and when it does we just have to deal with it. Does Elsie sleep?"

"She doesn't get through a whole night."

"Stan, you need help."

"I've told you," he said, crossly. "I won't put her in a home. She's looked after me for the last forty years. I won't turn my back on her now."

Jane allowed him to calm down before she continued.

"I meant maybe some respite care. If only for a few days. Maybe someone could come round in the afternoons to give you a break. It's too much for you to do on your own, Stan," she said, hoping she didn't sound like an awful nag. "You have the money, you know you do. You worked hard for it and that's what it's there for. Enough said."

Their meal arrived: a vegetable curry for her, duck for him.

"How's the detective agency?" he asked.

She told him about the search for Johnny's father – although she pretended it was for a client who lived elsewhere – the credit card case ("I'm due to start investigating that one in a day or two") and Lucy Erpingham, although again she changed the names and locations.

"I'm not surprised the girl's sister is worried about her. I wouldn't be able to sleep if Adele changed like that," she said.

"Why only one child, Jane?" Stan suddenly asked her. This wasn't a question he'd asked her before. "I remember you saying you wanted a brood."

"I did. Another one of life's setbacks, I'm afraid."

II

Jane hadn't needed to wait for the results of a pregnancy test to know she was pregnant. She'd known it from the moment she woke at four thirty a.m. and barely made it to the bathroom before she was sick.

The sickness continued throughout the morning. She called her mother, who turned up with a pregnancy test.

"It's positive," she yelled.

"I know," Jane replied from the floor, where she was kneeling in front of the toilet basin, preparing herself for another bout of retching.

"Morning sickness usually only lasts for twelve weeks dear," her mother said, sympathetically.

Jane was about to say: "Only?" when she was sick again.

"I'll make you a hot ginger toddy."

The brief respite she was granted when the morning sickness passed was quickly filled with sciatica.

"The baby is lying on a nerve, Mrs Hetherington," her midwife said. "You'll have to try and get him to move."

"I do and she just moves back again. When do I start blooming?"

"I hope I carry the next baby a lot easier than I'm carrying this one," she said to Hugh in bed that night.

"Let's see how we cope with this one before we start planning a second, eh?" Hugh muttered, trying to concentrate on the book in his hands – *Spinsters Become Suspicious* – the most recent of the Spinster Sister Sleuth Series. He'd met Jane when returning one of the series to the library for his mother. Back then, he'd thought the series asinine, but that was before he'd read one. Now he was an ardent fan.

"Three is a nice number," she said, ignoring her husband's comment and turning off her bedside lamp. "If this one is a boy, we can have a girl next, and vice versa; and then? ...Well, it won't matter what we have, if we already have one of each, will it? Maybe a little boy? Or another girl?" she mused.

Adele Julie Ann Hetherington was born at seven minutes past four on a Tuesday afternoon, weighing nine pounds. Her parents had been married for just under three years when she made her appearance.

Twenty-four hours after Adele's birth, Jane held the new-born infant in her arms, while her husband and parents sat by her hospital bed.

"She was born on a Tuesday," Jane said, cupping her baby's head in her hand. "She'll have far to go."

The consultant arrived. He was a kindly man, who understood the pain and disappointment his patients felt when trying to come to terms with the fact that their much-loved child would be the only biological one they would have. He understood this was a loss which could sometimes spill into an anger or a malaise, which could fester and grow over the years.

"You have a beautiful healthy daughter Jane, try focusing on that," he said. "All things being equal, you should be able to go home in a few days time. May I have a word with you Mr Hetherington and Mrs Preston?"

Jane didn't need to ask what the consultant wanted to speak to her husband and mother about, and said nothing as the three disappeared down the corridor towards the consultant's office. When finally alone with her father, and with Adele still cradled in her arms, she could no longer hold herself together and the tears came. He moved to sit on the bed beside her and put his arm around her.

"Let it out, love."

"It's not fair," she said, through her tears.

"Life's not fair, love."

"I wanted three children. I've always wanted three children."

"I know you did, love."

"Adele's going to be an only child."

"Your old dad's an only child, don't forget," he reminded her. "It's not the end of the world. If she's got your way with people, she'll be fine."

"It's not fair," Jane repeated, still in floods of tears.

"Jane, love, if you continue to dwell on what should have been, you'll waste your life away, pining for something you can't change. You must look to the future and plan your life around what you've got. You're not being fair to Hugh or Adele otherwise."

As he spoke, Jane sobbed softly.

"Don't allow yourself to wallow in self-pity. What's happened, has happened. Dwelling on it won't help anyone. So don't. Promise me, love," he said.

She looked up at her father and down at her daughter in her arms, who was beginning to stir.

"I'll try, Dad," she said, as bravely as she could manage.

In his office, the consultant spoke plainly to Jane's mother and husband.

"In our experience, some women are able to cope better in the situation that Jane finds herself in, than others. You should not underestimate the profound disappointment that Jane has undergone, as of course have you. I should warn you that she may be unable to prevent herself from dwelling on this. Also, we must not forget, she's undergone major and unexpected surgery, and all this combined with the normal hormonal changes women experience after childbirth…"

At that point, Jane's mother interrupted him. "Are you saying my daughter's likely to have a nervous breakdown?"

"No, Mrs Preston, I'm not, but I want you to remember that she may need more help than either of you are able to offer her. There is no shame in that. It won't do Adele any good to have a mother who is severely depressed. Just keep an eye on her. If things don't get better, or if they appear to be getting worse. If she can't cope, or she isn't enjoying the baby, come back and see us and we'll arrange for her to be referred to a psychiatrist, if we feel it necessary."

Edith Preston was quite annoyed at the consultant's suggestion that her daughter might need psychiatric help.

"She'll cope. She's a coper," she said angrily to Hugh on their way back to the ward.

Hugh himself was relieved to hear the doctor's words. He wasn't sure he could cope alone. He'd been in severe shock since a nurse had taken him to one side and said, "Your wife is haemorrhaging Mr Hetherington. We can't stop the bleeding. We're going to have to carry out a hysterectomy."

"But she's only twenty-six."

"I'm sorry."

Jane would have been the first to admit that the months which followed Adele's birth were some of the hardest of her life. Long after her physical wounds had healed, her emotions still see-sawed from the ecstasy of new motherhood, to mourning for the loss of her further children. Gradually though, she learned to cope with her mental scars as well as she ever would; and she and Adele slipped into an easy routine.

One day Jane took the baby out into the back garden. It was a warm day and there were swarms of tiny flies everywhere. She covered Adele's cot with a piece of lace, and sat beside her reading. Adele began to cough and Jane lifted the lace up off the cot and shook it. She looked down on her baby, who sneezed. Jane gently picked the baby up and returned to her seat with her in her arms. Adele looked as though she couldn't decide whether to cry or not. Jane supported the baby in her left arm and began to rock her to and fro.

"Daddy and I would have liked to have had more children, darling," she said to the child. "We wanted you to have brothers and sisters to play with. Someone who'd always be there for you, when Daddy and I are no longer around. But it wasn't to be. Your granddad said I wasn't to dwell on what can't be and I'm not going to. But I'm going to let you into a secret, darling, something even Daddy doesn't know. I'm going to tell you what your brother and sister would have been called. I would have called your brother Lachlan. I'm sure he would have taken after Daddy. He might have grown up to be an accountant too, or done something way out and rebellious like form his own band, and be famous – you never know. Your sister would have been called Pippa. I like to think she'd have been a cross between you and Lachlan; but mummy can't allow herself to think about it too much, because it makes her sad."

III

"I'm sorry Jane," Stan said, after she had shared this with him.

"I've long since made my peace with it," she said. "Dad was right. Brooding on what might have been would have been pointless and soul-destroying. I have my beautiful daughter and granddaughter, and another one on its way, not to mention all those years I had with Hugh. We must count our blessings in this life, Stan."

CHAPTER TWENTY-TWO

The Mouse Catcher General!

I

Jane woke early. After her nice evening out with Stanley, she'd slept surprisingly well. Although still only seven a.m. she didn't allow herself a lie-in. She'd returned home from the restaurant the night before to discover a note from Johnny pushed through her letterbox. The humane mouse trap had arrived, the note informed her. He'd set it up in her summerhouse, but she was to wait until the following morning before checking to see if it had an occupant.

She crossed a garden bathed in the first sun of the morning. A garden burgeoning into spring colour – the egg-yolk primroses, and the purple and pink Lenten roses, joining the snowdrops, narcissi and crocuses. She stopped to admire it – it was a joy to behold.

Johnny had left the humane mouse trap – a grey plastic rectangular box – in the middle of the floor. Jane picked it up. It didn't seem very heavy, but then mice didn't weigh very much. She gave it a little shake. She could tell immediately that there was something inside it. She could hear

scampering and squeaking. "Ha! Got you!" she said out loud.
She left the trap outside the back door. She'd have her breakfast,
then walk to the other side of town and release whatever was
inside.

Breakfast over, Jane left her house. Instead of walking into
Failsham as she would normally, she walked across the common, and from there took one of the many country lanes which
lead out of the town, where Johnny sometimes stood with his
sandwich board looking for work.

She walked along the lane until she reached some meadow
land. The walk had taken her about a quarter of an hour. The
meadow was surrounded by a stone wall to keep in the grey
horse which grazed there. To get over the wall and into the
meadow, Jane realised she was going to have to climb a stile.
At my age, she thought, as she lumbered over it with some dif-
ficulty. From the top of the stile she could see the broiler units
Johnny had helped to clean, looming large in the distance. The
horse cantered over to her. It gave a little nay and sniffed the
box in her hand.

"It's not an apple, I'm afraid," Jane said, stroking the horse's
head, and climbing down from the stile.

The two crossed the meadow together. At its far end, she
held the trap over a hedge, with the trap door facing downwards, and opened it. She gave it a shake, and after few minutes, the mouse fell out. The bewildered creature chased its tail
a few times before darting away to freedom. Jane peered inside
the trap. It was empty. Hopefully that's the end of that, she
thought.

As she walked along the lane in the direction of home, she
noticed a row of horseshoes nailed into the stone wall, one the

wrong way up. Although not unduly superstitious, she always righted upside down horseshoes, and this one would be no different. She leaned forward and took hold of one of its forks, but the horseshoe was quite stiff. She stepped up onto the grass verge to get closer and heard a twig snap beneath her foot, and felt her right shoe sink into something soft. Oh no, she thought removing her shoe. On closer examination she didn't find what she'd expected to, but play-dough.

Hmm, she said aloud, peeling the lump of multicoloured dough from the sole of her shoe. She put her shoe back on, still holding the dough. She looked down on the grass verge and saw a couple of play-dough stick people, holding hands. Very imaginative, she thought. She looked at the lump of play-dough in her hand. It could very well have been a stick person, before she'd stepped on it. With Felix's rant – Doesn't anyone know how to use a litter bin, these days! – clearly in her mind, she removed some tissues from her handbag, dropped the play-dough into it, and used the same tissues to pick up the stick people from the grass verge. She spotted a wheelie bin outside a nearby house, and deciding the children of the household had most likely made the play-dough shapes left by the roadside, she dropped the dough inside it before walking back into town.

II

From a table in a supermarket cafe, Jane studied Monty. He was much younger than Jane thought he'd be. She wouldn't have put him at more than twenty-five. She also thought she recognised him. Was he someone she'd met at the rally? The man at the ticket kiosk? One of the men they'd thought might be Pete Lambert? One of the baying mob?

"The more I think about it, the certainer I am that my Pete and yours is the same," Monty said. "I spoke to someone from the depot yesterday, and he thought it was as well. He backed up the Hull story. I could go and check it out for you?"

"I should really do that myself."

"You don't know no one there, like I do."

"What do you remember about Pete Lambert?"

"Not much, like I said. He kept himself to himself mostly. Just said he'd been married and had a kid, but he hadn't seen him for years."

"Did he say how many years?"

"May have done. Can't remember."

"Did he mention his son's name?"

"Yeah, but I couldn't tell you what it was."

Jane studied him. Whilst he was light on detail, nothing he'd said so far was wrong.

"Would you like to see the photo?" he asked.

Jane nodded. Monty pulled out a small photograph. In it, a group of men stood in two rows in front of a bus. Some waved to the camera, others gave a thumb's up, one a two-finger salute. "That's me," Monty said, pointing to the young man at the end of the first row. "And that's your man," he added, his finger resting just above a man in the middle of the second row.

Jane took the photograph and studied it. The man pointed out to her could well be Johnny's father, she realised. There was certainly a resemblance, although it wasn't striking, but given the size of the image, and the years which had passed between the taking of it, and the photographs Johnny had given her, this was unsurprising.

"It's him, isn't it?" Monty said, beaming.

"It could well be, Monty," she said, still staring at the photograph.

"Look. Let me go to Hull. I've got people I can stay with. I'll ask around. People know me. Someone is bound to know him if he's there. I might even bump into him. He's more likely to open up to me, than you."

After her phone conversation with Monty, Jane had searched against Pete Lambert and Hull, but once again had drawn a blank. This didn't mean he wasn't there, only he wasn't living there as Pete Lambert.

"'Course I'll need expenses…" Monty said.

While he talked on, Jane pondered. She didn't really want to fund Monty's reunion with his old Hull friends, although it sounded as though she was going to have to. Monty may really have worked with Pete Lambert, and he might actually know people in Hull who might be able to help him find Johnny's dad. That would be well worth the expense. She couldn't accompany him to Hull to keep an eye on him even if she'd wanted to (which she didn't – she barely knew him) because she was meeting Dean Moon the next day. Nonetheless she decided she was going to take the risk that she would never see Monty or her money again.

"Expenses?" she said.

"There's the cost of travel. I may 'ave to buy a few beers, slip some people a few tenners. A hundred should do it for starters."

It was a tidy sum, but not excessive, she thought. If he'd asked for a thousand pounds that would have been another matter. She took out four twenty pounds notes and two ten pounds notes and gave them to him.

"I'll call you the minute I got any news," he promised.

CHAPTER TWENTY-THREE

The Underwear Model

Johnny arrived at the photo shoot for the underwear catalogue escorted by Charity, who'd insisted on coming with him, even though her friends had said that when it came to male underwear catalogues, it wasn't other women she needed to worry about.

Charity looked around the studio – a camera, pointing at a blue screen – and whispered to Johnny, "Thought it would be a bit more glam, didn't you?"

"I was hoping for Bermuda," he replied, picking up the top garment of underwear – a pair of stretch hipsters – from a pile and holding it out to look at.

"We'll e-mail you the catalogue before it's published, in case any of the pictures compromise your dignity," the photographer promised.

"I don't have any of that, so there's nowt to worry about," Johnny replied, disappearing into the changing room to get changed into his first outfit, while Charity sat herself down in one of a row of chairs leaning against the wall. Minutes later Johnny pulled back the changing-room's curtains and stepped into the studio wearing the hipsters to applause from Charity and indifference from the photographer.

"The things I do for love," Johnny said.

The morning passed quickly. While Johnny posed in front of the blue screen wearing a succession of stretch slips, briefs, boxers, trunks and finally microskin long Johns ('for those cold winter nights', as the label put it) Charity gave herself a manicure, then settled down to read a book. Her friends had been right, she realised. She didn't have anything to be jealous about. The photo shoot was really rather boring, the tedium broken only by wondering what Johnny would emerge from the dressing room wearing next.

"I didn't realise there was so much choice in the world of male underwear," Charity said to the photographer, while Johnny darted back into the changing-room for his umpteenth change of the morning.

"We too have to dress to impress, nowadays," was the reply.

Johnny coughed loudly. Charity turned around to look, and burst out laughing. As Johnny, wearing what Charity would have described as a padded thong, and grinning from ear to ear, posed as Atlas.

"What on earth is that?" she asked.

"It's an enhancer," the photographer explained. "You're not the only ones who can make yourselves look younger and perkier then you really are, through the power of foam."

"Now this I must get a photo of," Charity said, getting up from her seat.

While the photographer took his selection of photographs, Charity took hers. "I think I've got everything I need and a bit more besides," she said, deciding to call it a day.

She gave Johnny a quick kiss goodbye and gave his enhancer a quick squeeze. From the street outside the photography studio, she sent the photos to everyone on her mailing list. The replies she received ranged from, 'Lucky you!' to 'Now I can die happy!'

CHAPTER TWENTY-FOUR

Charlie Moon

I

It was late afternoon by the time Jane arrived at Greenfields, the sheltered housing complex where Dean Moon's grandfather lived. She parked in the car park at its rear. Dean and his girlfriend, Liz, were waiting to greet her.

Once introductions were over, Dean said, "You're perfect for this job. You'll blend into the background nicely."

"Dean," Liz said, digging him in the rib cage.

Jane just laughed.

"I've just dropped Granddad off. I left him having a nap, thought we might start with a tour of Greenfields," Dean said.

"Good idea," Jane said.

The Greenfields sheltered housing complex was a collection of bungalows and studio apartments. Greenfields was large enough to allow every property in it to open onto its communal gardens, with the exception of those apartments on upper floors. These had balconies. The communal gardens formed the centrepiece of the complex. The complex and its gardens were well-tended: a sprinkler watered the lawn, bedding plants filled the flowerbeds and hanging baskets hung on either side of each front door. The pavements, which were lined with green handrails, were wide enough for wheelchairs to move across them easily, and the three could comfortably walk alongside each other as they strolled through the gardens. Greenfields was situated on top of a hill and Jane imagined the residents sitting out in this garden on a nicer day than this one, enjoying the panoramic views. What a lovely place to end one's days, she thought. When an elderly couple slowly shuffled by, arm in arm, Dean and Liz said hello, but Jane just felt a twinge of sadness.

"Granddad has one of those flats over there," Dean said, pointing to a row of two-storey apartments. "He's in one of the ground-floor ones. He's even got his own little patio."

"And one of those cords in case he has a fall," Liz added.

"Which he hasn't," Dean felt the need to point out. "Mum was so pleased when she got him in here, and now this has happened..." His words petered out.

The group stopped and sat down on a bench on the lawn.

"I believe there was something else you wanted to tell me?" Jane said. "Something you said you'd rather not put in an e-mail."

"The truth is..." Dean began, awkwardly. "The truth is my granddad's not quite the doddery old fool he makes himself out to be. I know my granddad, and it's not in his nature to take things lying down. I know damn well if he thinks someone has broken into his apartment, he'll be looking for them, and if he finds them..." Dean paused, before continuing, "I'm worried he's going to take matters into his own hands."

"You think he might be planning some form of revenge? Is that likely at his age?" Jane asked.

Dean and Liz glanced at each other.

"Highly likely," he said.

"When Dean's nan was still alive," Liz said. "She told me a family friend once had too much to drink at a party and propositioned her in the kitchen. She said that at first, Dean's granddad laughed it off and put it down to the drink; but a couple of months later, he and the man concerned spent the afternoon at the football and went for a drink afterwards, as though nothing had happened. She said that on the way home, Dean's granddad suddenly dragged his friend into an alleyway and beat the hell out of him. He said that if he ever touched his wife again, he'd kill him."

"He hasn't changed. If he thinks someone's done something to him, he won't forget it. He'll get even. He's old, but he's still as strong as an ox," Dean said.

"I see," said Jane. "Now I understand. You want me to try to discover who stole your grandfather's credit cards, before he does?"

"Exactly," Liz said, adding, "that's why we don't want to wait for the police to make an arrest either – might be too late by then."

"And should I manage to unmask the culprit, what will you do then?" Jane asked.

"You'll be visiting me in jail," Dean replied.

"Dean," Liz said.

"I'm only joking," he said. "I'll give their name to the police and let them deal with it."

"In which case, I'm delighted to accept your instructions. I think in the circumstances, I'd better start immediately, don't you? Could you remind me of your grandfather's name?"

"Charlie. Charlie Moon."

II

Jane drove to the hotel Liz had booked her into. She was there just long enough to freshen up. She wanted to be back at Greenfields in good time to join Granddad Moon and his fellow residents for a game of cribbage she knew was taking place that evening in the communal lounge.

She arrived back at Greenfields at just after half past six and made her way to the communal lounge. Ragtime music boomed out from inside the single story building. An unusual accompaniment for a quiet game of cribbage, she thought, throwing the fifty pence entrance fee into an upturned hat, smiling at the elderly gatekeeper, and stepping inside the lounge to find a casino in full swing. Gamblers dressed in outfits from the 1930s gathered around the twenty or so tables in the room to play roulette, blackjack or poker to a musical accompaniment provided by one of the residents playing a piano dressed as Al Capone. Jane scoured the lounge – there wasn't a game of cribbage in sight.

She looked around the room for Charlie Moon. As Charlie was the only man in the room with a moustache and a bright red bow tie and matching braces, she quickly found him sitting at a poker table, cards in front of him, and a drink to his right-hand side, which Jane guessed was stronger than lemonade. Seven Card Stud, it seemed, was Charlie's game.

A rather plump, rosy-cheeked woman lent against a long hatch, which separated the communal lounge from its kitchens, serving someone with a cup of tea and a slice of cake. Jane hadn't had time to eat, and she was rather hungry. She walked up to the counter and peered through the hatch into the kitchen where an array of goodies greeted her. She ordered a cup of tea and a cheese scone.

"I've not seen you before," the lady behind the hatch remarked.

"It was an impulse visit," Jane explained. "I am trying to decide if I'd like to take a bungalow eventually."

"It is always good to see a new face and a youngish one at that. Bea Applegate," Bea said, by way of introduction. "I live on site. Any questions – I'm the one to ask. Sugar?" she asked Jane, referring to the cup of tea she had just poured for her.

"No, thank you. And no butter on the scone either, thank you."

Bea looked slightly bewildered, then started to laugh.

"The average age of the regulars here is about eighty-five. At that age, no one counts calories any more."

While she waited for Jane to pay for her tea and scone, Bea continued chatting. "By yourself I see? Recently widowed, I'll wager?"

Jane pushed a one pound coin in the direction of Bea Applegate.

"Unfortunately I am, yes."

Bea took the money and dropped it into a tin box with a clatter. She wrote down the order in a notebook and, as she did this, she explained that she too was widowed.

"Some ten years now. It doesn't get any easier. Working here helps, though. Not everyone here is as independent as they look. Some are in and out of each other's houses all the time, but some would never see anyone if it wasn't for me and my staff. We help them with their shopping, prescriptions, finances, filling in forms and the like, but if all they want is someone to talk to, then we're there for that as well," she said, proudly.

Jane wondered how much money Bea earned working here. Probably not very much, and her staff even less. The temptation to exploit elderly, sometimes confused people, might be more than some could resist.

"Events like this must cheer the residents up. Wouldn't do any harm if the stakes were a bit higher, though, would it?" Jane said, having noticed that the residents were gambling with dummy money.

"But we'd need a gambling licence for that. What people do behind their front doors is their business, but we can't have them openly gambling on the premises – we'd get shut down."

Jane left Bea serving two elderly ladies. She decided her best course of action would be quiet observation, and therefore sat down quietly at Charlie Moon's poker table. Although women outnumbered men in the room, two men and a woman were Charlie Moon's opponents at the table. The stakes may have been oversized, vividly coloured fake-banknotes, but those at the table played as though the stakes were high. Jane found the intensity and competitiveness of the game, whose competitors only took their eyes off each other to check their cards, or count out their money before moving it to the centre of the table, fascinating.

"Betsy?" the dealer asked. The dealer, a man who could have been anywhere between seventy and eighty-five, was wearing a green visor.

The two of diamonds lay face up in front of Betsy. It was the lowest ranked card on the table. The other cards on display were the two of hearts, the king of spades and the ten of clubs. Betsy appeared to be something of a cardsharp. She stared at the two cards in her hand before placing them face-down on the table in front of her and said, "I'll open fifty pounds, Ted, I mean dealer."

Granddad was next. He matched Betsy's stake and slipped his arm around her shoulder. "I once played in a mob game, you know. It was in Cuba, in 1958."

"Who won, Charlie?" Betsy asked.

Charlie chuckled. "Well, as I'm still alive fifty years later, who do you think won?"

"Horace?" dealer Ted asked the largest player at the table. He, too, matched Betsy stake, as did Ted.

"Right. Third round, dealer," Horace said.

Ted, the dealer, obliged. He dealt each player in turn three cards, each dealt face-up on the table. On sight of his third card, the four of diamonds, Horace folded.

"Match you and raise you," Ted said, throwing some notes of indeterminable currency into the centre of the table. Betsy lifted up the corner of her cards and checked her hand again. She, too, threw more notes into the pot. Now it was Charlie Moon's turn to snort in disgust.

"I'll raise you," he said.

Ted glowered at him. "You're bluffing."

"We'll see whether I am or not, you senile old fool," Granddad Moon retorted.

"Gentlemen please," interjected Horace. "Final card, dealer," he said.

Ted dealt each player their final card, this time the cards were placed face-down on the table. When the final round of dealing was over, Ted shot Granddad Moon, a long disdainful look, before turning to ask Betsy if she was still in. When Betsy hesitated, her portly neighbour grew impatient.

"If you don't mind, woman, I'd like this poker game to finish before I meet my maker, which at my age may not be too far away."

"You leave her alone, Horace," Charlie warned. As he spoke, he leant closer to Horace.

"I second that," said Ted.

"I think I'm out," Betsy remarked, seemingly oblivious to the protective feelings she was generating around the table.

Jane couldn't help wondering whether all this friendly rivalry was itself a bluff. Was the thief sat at this table, falsely confident that he or she had escaped suspicion, while all the time Charlie was searching him out, ready to pounce when he had? Jane could understand Dean's concern. Charlie Moon was elderly, but so were the other residents and Charlie looked taller and stronger than many in the room, including some of the staff, and, of course, it wasn't the size of the dog in the fight that counted.

Across the table, Charlie Moon and the dealer turned away from Horace and towards each other instead.

"You in or out?" Ted asked.

"Out! With my hand?" Charlie Moon said, throwing yet more money into the pot.

Ted clucked and adjusted his visor and matched Charlie's stake, muttering, "Let's see what you've got, old man."

The two of hearts, the Queen and seven of clubs and the Jack of spades were in view. With a triumphant snort, Charlie turned over his cards to reveal another queen, a king, and the five of hearts. Betsy squealed excitedly to survey and clapped loudly.

"Your turn, Ted," she said.

"Your turn, Ted," Charlie mimicked, sarcastically.

Unfortunately, Ted's hand turned out to consist of nothing of significance and the winnings were all Charlie's. As though to add salt to the wound, Charlie insisted on counting out the notes.

"Three hundred and seventy-five pounds," he said, holding the fake currency out for all to see. "Horace is down ninety pounds, Betsy one hundred and five pounds and Ted one hundred and eighty pounds. Are we agreed? Now, how about we get ourselves a nice cup of tea and a slice of Battenburg, followed by a game of blackjack, Betsy?"

"Oh that would be lovely, Charlie," she replied.

Ted said nothing and beside him Horace chuckled. No one who saw it could have missed the look on Ted's face as Charlie and Betsy made their way, arm in arm, over to the tea counter. Jane saw it. So did Horace. He'd seen the jealousy in Ted's eyes and for some reason it made him laugh. Were Charlie and Ted rivals for Betsy's affections, Jane wondered. If they were, this could only complicate matters, by making revenge or jealousy another possible motive for the theft. Dear me, thought Jane. This was all getting very convoluted.

"All this excitement isn't good for my pacemaker," Horace said, getting up from the table. With a nod in Jane's direction, he walked over to the door and left. Bea walked over to Jane and began collecting the empty cups.

"Enjoying yourself?" asked Bea.

Jane nodded.

"If you'd like to play, ask the Culleys, they organised it."

"The Culleys?"

"Ted and Betsy."

"They're married?" Jane said, rather surprised.

"Almost fifty-five years, I hear."

"Good Lord!"

Charlie and the Culleys eventually left together, followed by Jane.

Outside the building, Dean's granddad turned to walk one way and the Culleys another, but before they parted company, Charlie said to Ted,

"I'll be at your place by mid-day."

No one seemed perturbed by these words and as the Culleys turned left, Charlie turned right. Despite the slowness of his years, his stride was steady and purposeful and it didn't take him too long to reach his ground-floor flat. He slowly opened his door and disappeared inside it. Jane thought she should wait awhile, in case he reappeared. Although it was still relatively early, she wasn't sure where she should wait. There was a bench nearby, but Jane was slightly worried about drawing attention to herself. This, after all, was sheltered accommodation, and she was concerned that one of the staff might see her sitting on a bench alone in the dark and believe she'd forgotten who or where she was. This, she supposed, was why most private detectives smoked. It gave them a convincing reason for being outside alone at any time of the day or night. One side of the bench was lit by a street lamp. Jane sat at the other, camouflaged by darkness, wondering how long she was going to be there. Her knitting was at the hotel, as was her book, not that she could see well enough to do either, anyway. She began to wish she'd taken the leap and bought herself the Smartphone she was considering buying. At least she could have tested her heartbeat and blood pressure while she waited.

She noticed that there weren't any lights on in the flat next door to Charlie's. Hopefully, this meant its owners were either out or asleep. She stepped into their porch and waited. She wasn't sure what she would do if they returned and found her there, but luckily this wasn't to be a problem, for, after only about fifteen minutes, she heard the door to Charlie's flat open and shut again and a few minutes after that the old man walked past her. He'd changed his shirt and was holding a beautifully wrapped present, complete with a large gold bow. Jane watched Charlie stop at the door of the flat two away from his, and knock on it. While he waited for the door to open, Jane studied his strong, chiselled features and mane of white hair. What a good-looking man he must have been when young, she thought.

The door was opened by a woman Jane had seen in the communal lounge earlier on. Other than a cursory nod in each other's direction, she hadn't seen the two speak, but they were certainly talking now, and more. Charlie had thrown his arms around his lady-friend's shoulders and was kissing her. Only when the kissing stopped did he hand her his present. This time she kissed him. Eventually, the couple stepped into her flat and the door closed behind them. If they'd been younger, Charlie would have carried her inside, Jane thought. Liz had already told her that Charlie had once been something of a ladies' man. In his younger days, he'd 'run Dean's nan a merry dance,' she'd said. Some things never change, thought Jane.

As it appeared unlikely she would see Granddad Moon again that evening, she decided to return to her hotel.

Once back in her hotel room, and after telephoning room service and asking them to send up a selection of sandwiches, she sat down at the desk, opened her ruled shorthand notepad, and compiled a list of suspects:

Bea Applegate
Unknown staff member(s)
Ted Cully
Betsy Cully
Horace
Woman in flat
Unknown resident(s)
None of the above

Jane closed her eyes. This was getting ridiculous. She'd been on the case for less than twenty-four hours and so far, all she had to show for it was an ever-expanding list of suspects. When Jane had decided to become a private detective she'd been worried about many things, one being whether she'd be able to solve every case. Here, it wasn't so much a matter of solving the case, but of being able to do so before the guilty party was hospitalised by the victim, and it caused her great concern.

CHAPTER TWENTY-FIVE

The Real McCoy

I

Jane returned to Greenfields for eleven thirty a.m. Although she'd heard Charlie arrange to call in on the Culleys at midday, she hadn't thought to establish where the Culleys actually lived. She decided to wait for Charlie to emerge from whichever flat he'd spent the night in and follow him to the Culleys' place. She chose a bench at the far side of the gardens, which faced Charlie's flat and from which she could also see the majority of Greenfields, including the infamous communal lounge. Behind her was the car park, where two young lads took it in turns to skateboard.

She hadn't been waiting long, when she saw Charlie leave his flat and walk over to the car park. The minute he came into view, the two boys stopped skateboarding and started to walk in his direction. Charlie and the two boys converged in the car park, watched on by Jane. The two boys positioned themselves on either side of the old man. A few words were said, but Jane couldn't hear anything of the conversation. Charlie produced his wallet and handed one of the boys what looked like quite a lot of money. More words were said and the money pocketed by the boys. One of the two lads jumped on his skateboard, and using his left leg to project himself, skateboarded away with his companion running by his side.

"Oi!" Charlie called out. The two boys stopped and looked back. Charlie Moon pointed at his watch, held up five fingers in the air, and yelled, "My place."

Charlie certainly didn't appear to be either shaken, nor upset; in fact, quite the opposite. Jane, however, was on her feet. Charlie had clearly handed a large sum of money over to one of the skateboarders. For heaven's sake, she thought. What on earth did he do that for? Had they made him?

She wondered if she should call Dean or run after the boys. Even if that had been going to practical, it was now too late – the lads had disappeared from sight. She looked over to Charlie. Wherever he was going next, he clearly wanted to look his best for it. He'd produced a mirror from his pocket, placed it on the bonnet of a car, and was combing his hair. He spat into his hand and used his saliva to wet down his hair. Finally, he straightened his tie and collar before returning both mirror and comb to his pocket. He set off towards his rendezvous, followed by Jane.

Despite his frailty, he was still putting up a good pace. He left the car park and retraced his steps, only this time he continued past the apartment block which housed his flat, to a row of bungalows set back from it. He stopped at the first property and marched up the driveway and began hammering at the door. Although Jane was still some way from him, she could hear him hollering.

"Open up, old dears! Open up! Open up!" he yelled, still hammering at the front door.

The front window opened and Betsy's head appeared.

"Get that old man out of bed," Charlie demanded. "Tell him I'm here. I said I'd be here at mid-day, and I'm here."

Jane glanced at her watch. It was twelve thirty-one.

"Ted!" Betsy yelled. "Ted, Charlie's here." This conversation too, was conducted at full volume.

Betsy's head disappeared back inside the window, but before she had time to shut it, Charlie bellowed out, "I've come for my winnings."

Betsy's head reappeared at the window. "Keep your voice down, will you? You'll have us evicted."

"There's no one around to hear us, woman," Charlie retorted angrily. "There's only two of 'em on duty and they'll both be watching soap operas."

After a few minutes the front door opened and Ted appeared, still wearing his dressing gown. "Two hundred and eighty-five quid," Charlie stated. "That's what I won and I'm here to collect it."

Two hundred and eighty-five pounds, thought Jane. She opened her notebook and quickly checked her notes. Betsy had lost one hundred and five pounds to Charlie the night before and her husband one hundred and eighty pounds, making two hundred and eighty-five pounds in total. It looked as though Charlie was here to collect it, only this time it wasn't fake money he wanted. He'd come for the real McCoy. Well, well, well, thought Jane. No wonder things were so heated at the poker table. Jane could only admire the ingenuity of it all. Not only did the residents get around the ban on gambling for cash - but they did so under the eyes of the staff, which could only add to the sense of satisfaction.

"Tell Betsy to fetch my money," Charlie instructed Ted, still standing in the doorway. "Everyone knows you keep your money under the bed, you damned fool. And get a move on, man. I've a taxi arriving any minute now."

Jane didn't need to hear any more. She decided to try and intercept the taxi.

She found it waiting, its engine humming. "I wonder if I could ask you directions?" she asked the driver. "If you have time? Are you waiting for someone?"

"I'm waiting to take one of the old boys to the bookies, but he's not here yet, so fire away," the taxi driver replied. He was a young man with a shaved head and tattooed knuckles.

Jane told the driver that she had to drive to a nearby town the following day and was wondering which, of two routes, to take. Despite his appearance the young taxi driver turned out to be extremely helpful and began by informing her immediately which of the two routes she certainly shouldn't choose.

"Been single lane for six frigging months now. Don't think I've seen a frigging workman yet. Seen enough frigging cones mind you," he complained, unconcerned that his language might offend. "Here he is, here's my ride," the driver said, when Charlie came into view. Jane looked across the car park to see Charlie crossing it in his usual slow, but regal manner.

"A regular?" Jane said.

"I'll say," the driver replied. "I'd go bust if it wasn't for old Charlie's trips to the bookies. Not to mention all those fancy restaurants you take your lady-friends to, eh Charlie?" he said just as the man himself reached the taxi. The taxi driver stepped out of his car to open the door for Charlie. "We'll never keep you away from the ladies or the horses, will we old boy?" the driver said to Charlie, with a large grin.

Charlie chuckled to himself and climbed into the car, muttering, "Less of the old from you, laddy."

"I'm going into town, would you mind very much if I shared your taxi and we split the fare?" Jane asked Charlie.

"I'd be more than delighted to share my taxi with such a beautiful young woman," Charlie Moon replied, indicating for Jane to climb into the taxi next to him. "I wouldn't dream of expecting you to split the fare."

"That's most kind of you," Jane said, stepping into the taxi and sitting next to him on the back seat.

"We'll treat it as a first date," he said, giving her hand a quick squeeze.

In his car mirror, the taxi driver gave Jane a wink, and the taxi moved off.

"What big hands you have," Jane said. "Were you ever a boxer?"

"Junior amateur champion: welterweight. Under twenty-one amateur champion: welterweight. Army amateur champion: welterweight. I was a left-paw," he said, punching the air with his left hand. "I don't box officially any more, you understand. I'm too old. I could still take on half these youngsters, though," he said with a mischievous laugh. The driver laughed but Jane didn't, because she was quite sure he could.

The taxi pulled to a stop at the rank in the town centre, where Jane got out. Charlie remained in the back of the vehicle, searching through his pockets for the fare. Jane had seen a poster advertising a dance taking place that evening at the communal lounge, and after waiting for Charlie to settle the fare said, "I hope you don't find it presumptuous my asking you this, Charlie, but I wondered if you were going to the dance this evening?"

The driver burst out laughing. "Mind out, love – he's seventy-nine! You trying to kill him off?"

"I'm seventy-eight and five quarters!" Charlie yelled, climbing out of the car. "My, you're a forward one, lady. Matter of fact, I am going to the dance, yes, but I already have a date or two." He took her hand and gave it a little squeeze. Although his fingers were bony and his skin wrinkled, there was still some strength left in the old man's grip. "But I'll still find time for a dance with you, my lovely, I promise you that."

Jane turned to walk away, then stopped and spun around. Charlie, who was waiting for his change, stopped to look up at her, as did the taxi driver.

"I wonder if...Oh dear, this is a bit embarrassing," she said, covering her mouth with her hand, and attempting to look as embarrassed as she could. "I don't normally do things like this," she said, coquettishly. The taxi driver and Charlie looked at each other and then back to Jane, clearly wondering what on earth she was going to say. "It's just, maybe, we could meet up for a coffee later this afternoon," she blurted out.

"Cor blimey, Charlie," the taxi driver said. "Wish I had your way with the ladies."

"I'm free at five today," she said, playfully.

"I'm meant to be back for..." he started to say. Jane knew he was referring to the five o'clock meeting she'd seen him arrange with the youngsters. Would she prove a bigger draw than they? "What the heck," he said. "It can wait. What's more important than coffee with a beautiful woman?"

"Five it is then," Jane said, as the taxi driver rolled his eyes and shook his head.

"I believe there's a coffee shop in there," she said, pointing to a department store nearby. She hadn't a clue whether there was a coffee shop there or not, but as she had no intention of meeting Charlie for coffee anyway, it was an academic point.

"Okay," Charlie said. "Five p.m. for coffee it is."

Jane even managed to giggle girlishly before they separated.

Jane waited for a few minutes then doubled back on herself. Charlie had departed in the direction of the High Street. Jane caught up with him, still making his way slowly, but purposefully along the street. She hung back. She didn't want Charlie to turn around and see her, but she needn't have worried. Charlie looked straight ahead until he reached the bookies and went inside. Jane could imagine everyone there shouting his name out as he stepped inside.

After waiting a while she peered through the windows of the bookies as discreetly as she could. The windows were darkened and Jane could see very little and gave up. Other than the occasional sweepstake on the Grand National, Jane herself had never really gambled, nor had Hugh. However, she knew what the inside of a betting shop looked like, and assumed there would be so many people inside it that Charlie wouldn't be able to beat somebody up in there, even if he'd wanted to. She looked at her watch. It was ten past one in the afternoon. Did he intend gambling for hours? Quite possibly, she thought.

Left with no choice but to hang around and find out, she bought herself a newspaper from a nearby newsagents, and settled down on the bench at the end of the road. She waited and waited and waited. She'd read the paper from cover to cover, finished the Sudoku, the Codeword, and was two thirds of the way through the Crossword, when Charlie emerged from the betting shop, grinning. He must have won, she thought.

She looked at her watch. It was five past four. She realised Charlie was walking in her direction, and quickly concealed herself behind the newspaper, waiting for him to pass her. As he did, she took out her compact and opened it and pretended to powder her face. In the compact's mirror, she watched Charlie make his way down the street. With the mirror still open, she quickly ran her fingers through her hair, snapped the mirror closed, dropped it back into a handbag, and got up to follow him. When Charlie reached a barbers, he disappeared from sight. She looked through its window and nearly jumped out of her skin. Charlie had someone in a headlock. Good Lord. Should she intervene? Once again, she had no need to worry. Charlie quickly released his captive, a man no younger than him, and the two men began a play fight, which ended with Charlie putting his hands up in mock surrender. The other party to the fight left the barbers shortly afterwards, laughing and waving goodbye to Charlie and the barber.

Jane watched Charlie settle himself down in the barber's chair while the barber threw a towel around him and made ready to shave him. Jane glanced at her watch again. It was now ten past four, giving Charlie enough time for a haircut and a shave, before meeting her at five o'clock. She could only hope he'd wait for her at the coffee shop for at least thirty minutes, before giving up on her. Given the time it would then take him to get back to Greenfields again, this should give her more than enough time to complete her business there.

She left Charlie Moon at the barbers, and got a taxi back to the sheltered accommodation complex, where she hurried to Charlie's flat to await the skateboarders' return. They arrived on cue at exactly five o'clock, both on foot, although one held his skateboard under his arm. The other clutched a plastic bag. Jane walked over to meet them. Neither boy made any attempt to run away.

"Okay, love?" one of the two boys asked her.

"Are you expecting Charlie Moon," Jane asked. "If so, I'm afraid he's just telephoned me to say he's running late. He won't be here for at least an hour."

"What?" one of the boys said.

"We were meant to be having coffee. I was so looking forward to it," Jane said, with the sigh.

The boys looked at each other, clearly annoyed.

"Told you we should get him a mobile phone," one said to the other.

"What we going to do? I ain't waiting," his friend replied.

"Maybe I can pass on a message?" Jane said.

"You one of his girlfriends?" the first boy asked Jane, suspiciously.

"Well, I wouldn't go that far," Jane said. "But we are very good friends."

"What we meant to do with this?" one demanded of the other holding the plastic bag aloft.

"I'll ensure he gets it," Jane said. "It'll give me a nice excuse to call round."

One of the boys looked at her with a mixture of pity and mild contempt, while the others said, "Yeah – give her the stuff – I ain't coming back again this evening."

The other boy wasn't so certain that Jane was to be trusted.

"We can't just give her his stuff."

"It's his fault if he's not here," the first said indignantly. He turned to Jane and said, "If you don't mind, love?" holding the plastic bag out to her.

She took it. As she did, the boy grabbed the other by the arm and said, "Come on."

The two turned on their heels and walked away, whispering conspiratorially to themselves, turning around now and then to stare at Jane. She gave them a few minutes after they had disappeared from sight, before returning to her car, which she'd parked some way from Greenfields.

Once there, she looked inside the plastic bag the boys had given her. She found ten packets of tobacco in plastic pouches, which she presumed were probably smuggled. There was also a sealed white A5 envelope. Jane very carefully opened it, taking care not to damage the seal, so she could reseal it if necessary. She took out the contents and stared at them. The envelope contained a new driver's licence. The photograph on the plastic card was of Charlie Moon, but the name and address on it weren't his, nor the date of birth, unless he was only fifty-three. The card was clipped on to a gas bill and a statement of annual earnings, giving Charlie Moon an annual income considerably higher than the state pension he actually got. Both the gas bill and the statement of earnings were addressed to a person of the same name and address as that appearing on the fake driver's licence.

"Oh," Jane said to herself, continuing to stare at the paperwork in her hand. "Oh dear me," she said, realising the envelope contained a completely new I.D for Charlie Moon. A false I.D would allow him to obtain credit cards and run up balances which he would never need to pay back. Unlike the last time. Then he'd nearly been caught. He'd had to think on his feet when the threatening letters arrived, cleverly pretending to be the victim, and probably because of his age, everyone had believed him. A few others had maintained they too had been the victims of crime. Maybe they had been, or maybe they too had spent more money than they cared to repay.

Charlie couldn't keep doing that every time he needed money. He needed someone to help create a false I.D, which wouldn't lead the police straight to his door. The boys, she presumed, were go-betweens for professional criminals. People who could get anybody anything they wanted. Jane couldn't be certain how Charlie Moon had come across them, but in the circles he moved in, it wouldn't have been that difficult. Once the new bank account was opened, a debit or credit card would be delivered to the false address. From there, it would be run over to Charlie's flat. He'd withdraw the money over a few weeks and spend it over a few months. From what Jane had seen and been told about Charlie Moon, she suspected that in his younger days, he hadn't been a stranger to crime. She doubted he was concerned about the police catching up with him, if they ever did. He knew he was unlikely to be sent to jail for very long at his age, so what did he care?

Jane slipped the paperwork back into the envelope and carefully resealed it. She couldn't give it to Charlie Moon, so what could she do with it? Pass it over to his grandson and let him take care of it, she decided.

II

She didn't go straight home, but decided to return to Greenfields for the start of the evening dance. She wanted to see Charlie's entrance. She hid from view, and waited.

Charlie was one of the last to arrive and when he did, dressed in a dark tuxedo, blue bow tie and matching cummerbund, he did so triumphantly escorting not one, but two women, as elderly as he, both wearing long evening dresses and clutching a single red rose. This sight caused Jane to say,

"And I was worried my best was over!"

III

While she sat in her car outside the drab tower block where Dean Moon and Liz lived, Jane thought back over the events of the last few days. A downside to her job was the unpredictability of her clients' reaction when she unearthed something they really didn't want to hear. This had happened to her the previous month, when a client didn't care to learn what Jane had discovered. The same dilemma faced her again as she wondered how to tell Dean about his grandfather's 'double life'. Would he even believe her?

In the living room of a flat much nicer than the concrete tower block which contained it, Jane calmly told Dean and Liz everything she'd learned, before passing the envelope over to them to read. They stared at its contents for some time.

"What made him to it?" Dean asked eventually.

"It's quite simple," Jane said. "He needed the money. I've spent the last two days following your grandfather, and I can tell you that he's doing his damnedest to live life to the full, as much of the constraints of age will allow him to, but unfortunately he can't afford it. I very much doubt he considers himself as a criminal."

"Yeah, but the police will," Dean pointed out. "I'm going to pay granddad a visit this evening and tell him I know what he's up to and if he doesn't stop it, I'll put him in an old people's home under twenty-four-hour supervision," he went on, pointing his finger at Jane. "That'll clip his feathers."

"At least we don't have to worry about the police ringing us up to say they've arrested your granddad for grievous bodily harm," Liz said.

"Let's wait to see how he reacts to what I'm going to tell him this evening before we say that, eh?" Dean replied.

Jane left happy. One case down – two to go.

CHAPTER TWENTY-SIX

Cauliflowers and Cabbages

I

Jane woke up the next morning with one task in mind. Her stake-out of Charlie Moon had convinced her that she needed more than just the bog-standard mobile phone she currently used. She needed a Smartphone. A small shop just off the Market Square (run by a local man, a few years older than her daughter) sold such gadgets. She set off for the shop.

On her way there she passed an estate agency. She studied the properties displayed in the agent's window. Old Jimmy Anderson's bungalow was on the market, she noted. The photograph of his bungalow brought a smile to her lips as she remembered the morning, almost thirty years earlier, when she'd come across Jimmy, then well into his eighties, standing on a pair of stepladders, propped up on the footpath outside his front garden, trimming his yew hedge with a pair of handheld hedge trimmers.

II

As always, thirty-four-year-old Jane Hetherington was dressed in the height of fashion. She wore a high ruff-necked, long-sleeved lace blouse and a lambswool jumper, over an ankle-length tweed skirt. For the first time in her life she'd taken to wearing flats. She still didn't like them, but they were Lady Di's favourite footwear, so what was a girl to do? A simple row of pearls and a velvet headband completed the outfit.

"How are you Jimmy?" Jane asked him.

"Someone keeps stealing my vegetables, that's how I am," he replied, climbing down from the step ladder to face Jane.

Jimmy grew vegetables in his own back garden and sold them to passing motorists from a small stall erected in his front garden.

"Soon as I step out in front, they steal from the back. They're probably there now, stealing. But soon as I leave the front garden and go to the back, they steal from the front!"

"What about the money in the honesty-tin?" Jane asked, referring to the small tin he sometimes left on the stall in the front garden, to allow passers-by to purchase vegetables if it was unattended.

"Untouched," he said. "This carries on, I'll be leaving them vegetables to rot in the ground, Mrs Hetherington. You've got a good head on your shoulders. See if you can find the culprit. If you do, you can have free cauliflowers for the rest of your life," he promised.

Jane wanted to help. She was also intrigued by the unusual nature of the crime. She agreed to take on the case.

When Jane picked Adele up from school that day, she told her all about the bad people who were stealing from old Jimmy.

"They shouldn't do that," Adele said. "Stealing is very naughty."

"It most certainly is," her mother agreed, Adele's tiny hand in hers. "If mummy can find the bad men doing it, she'll get given lots of cauliflowers by Uncle Jimmy."

"Cauliflower cheese for tea every night, yippee!" squealed Adele. Cauliflower cheese was her favourite meal.

"You must help him. Poor old bugger," Hugh said later on, after Jane told him of her conversation with Jimmy. "It's bad enough him trying to struggle on alone, at his age, without all this."

Jimmy's wife had predeceased him some two years earlier, leaving him a widower at the age of seventy nine. The couple had no children. Jane could still remember her Memorial service. "I don't know what I'm going to do without her," Jimmy had said to Jane and Hugh. "I really don't. I feel like my right arm's been cut off."

Jane visited old Jimmy the next morning. She began by asking him to show her the scene of the crime.

"Crimes," he reminded her.

They walked around to the back garden. His property was the last on the street. The empty property next to his was for sale.

"They still not found a buyer for that property yet?" Jane asked.

"The agents think the couple who looked round yesterday are going to make an offer. It'll be nice to have neighbours again," he said.

Jimmy's back garden was long and narrow. Unlike the bungalow next door, Jimmy's property hadn't been extended, and it was almost half the size of the neighbouring property. It still had a septic tank in the back garden. Most of the garden was laid to lawn, and the few flowerbeds which remained were overrun with weeds, or hugely overgrown shrubs which had been allowed to run wild. As well as the septic tank, there was a large shed, a broken greenhouse, and a derelict chicken coop in the back garden. The majority of the greenhouse windows were broken and tall weeds were sprouting where plants would once have been cultivated. The lawn was overgrown in patches and bare in others. It was obvious that things had become too much for Jimmy and he couldn't cope. He must have noticed the look on Jane's face.

"The garden's really too much for me at my age," he confided.

"I'm sure Hugh would be only too happy to run the lawn mower over the lawn for you, Jimmy. That'll keep the grass down at least, and I'm sure I can find the time to tend flower beds for you," she added.

There was one area of the garden, however, where Jimmy could be justifiably proud and that was his vegetable plot. This he tended night and day. Raspberries and runner beans grew alongside onions, carrots, potatoes, cabbages and cauliflowers.

"It's only the cabbages and cauliflowers that keep being nicked," Jimmy explained. "Whoever keeps taking stuff ain't interested in the little vegetables, as I call 'em, only the cauliflowers and cabbages, although I grow all of them, as you know. Strange thing is, the thieving doesn't happen all the time. Just now and then, early evenings and weekends mostly. And only when it's still light. Never night, when you'd expect a thief to strike."

"I see," Jane said, even though as yet she didn't. She didn't at all.

Jane and Jimmy made their way to the front garden. This had been turned over to gravel some years earlier, although weeds poked through, even so. Jimmy sold his produce from a table covered with a cloth, protected by a gazebo. Jimmy's bungalow faced a fairly busy road and for as long as anyone could remember, Jimmy had piled his stall high with whatever he'd produced that year, and sold it to locals and passers-by. Many stopped at his stall to purchase its produce, truthfully marketed as having been picked that day. Sometimes, he'd even walk his customers around to his vegetable plot at the back of the house and harvest his produce for them there and then. Once, he'd sold newly laid eggs from his brood of chickens, but the chickens had stopped laying at about the time his wife passed away, and he'd given them away to a good retirement home, to, as he put it, 'live out their old age in comfort'.

"They were always her girls," he'd said at the time. "If they couldn't lay for her no more, they weren't going to lay for no one no more."

Jane studied the terrain. Jimmy's bungalow was set a little way back from the road. On the opposite side of the road where Jimmy lived, there was open farmland – an easy escape route, she thought. The back garden had once been surrounded by the same yew hedge that grew in the front, but that had been ripped up years ago and replaced by a wooden fence. The property backed on to a quiet lane. The lane led back to the town centre, as did the road at the front of the house. The back garden was overlooked by trees. Jane noticed sand spread out in front of the fence. When she asked why it was there, Jimmy admitted to putting it down in the hope that he might find a footprint left in it, but none had been. Jane walked over to peer at the sand. It was undisturbed. The thieves were getting in and out another way.

They moved inside his kitchen.

"Tell me more about the crimes, Jimmy," she said, a pot of tea brewing on the table. Jane donned a pair of rubber gloves she'd bought with her, and started working her way through what must have been a month's worth of washing-up piled up in the sink and the surrounding worktops. Jimmy dried up. In no time, it was done.

"Things have got on top of me, Mrs Hetherington," he admitted. "What with me missus passing away and now all of this thieving."

Jane poured him a mug of tea and sat him down at the table. She glanced around the kitchen. When Jimmy's wife had still been alive, the house had been spotless. Anybody could literally have eaten their dinner off the floor. Not so now. It was filthy and cluttered. It was no good, she'd have to come back again and tackle the grime before it got out of hand. An afternoon should do it, she thought, wondering how much food he had in his fridge and resolving to return later with a casserole. "You're managing very well, Jimmy," she said, opening a packet of digestive biscuits she'd bought on the way, and offered them to him. "Now, let's get back to these missing cauliflowers of yours."

"And cabbages," he reminded her.

"Cauliflowers and cabbages. Tell me everything you know about the crimes, Jimmy."

Jimmy helped himself to three of the biscuits. He dunked one in the tea and ate it. The most recent crime had happened at about four in the afternoon, the day before last, he explained. A family of four had seen a sign he'd put up, offering fresh runner beans for sale, and had stopped to purchase some. Jimmy had taken the family around to his back garden, leaving a cauliflower, cut only an hour before, on the stall. The family had picked as many runner beans as they'd wanted, while Jimmy had dug up some potatoes and onions. As he spoke, Jane took notes. When Jimmy and the family returned to the front garden, they found the cauliflower gone, but the honesty-tin and the money in it, untouched. As with the previous incidents, there was no sign of anyone nearby. "The worst part about it, Jane, was that when I returned to the back garden, a cabbage had been stolen from there too. It had still been there when I'd been in the back garden with the family. They must have taken a cabbage when we were in the front garden, having gone and pinched the cauliflower when we were in the back. When we were in the back garden, they were in the front, and when we were in the front, they were in the back. I can't see how none of us saw or heard anything," he said, shaking his head in disbelief. "I wouldn't have minded too much, Jane, I grow more than I need, but I'd promised that cabbage to old Mrs Flaxman up the road."

"I think there must be more than one thief, Jimmy," Jane said, tapping a ballpoint pen against her lips, sagely. "No thefts since?"

He shook his head. "Nothing's gone missing since then."

"I see," she said, even though she still didn't. "To solve a crime, Jimmy, one needs to understand it. By that I mean, one needs to understand both methodology and motive. One often leads to the other, I find. Do you mind if we take another stroll around the property, Jimmy?"

Minutes later he and Jane were walking along the narrow country lane which ran behind his house. Properties lined one side, a hedgerow the other, then fields. In the field nearest to the lane, a herd of cows were grazing. "Used to walk my old dog along here," Jimmy said "when we were both nippers, relatively speaking."

A young couple who lived in the town were coming the other way. They stopped to talk to Jane and Jimmy. "Find out who's taking your cabbages yet, old boy?" the young man asked.

"Not yet, but expecting to any minute, now I've called in the big guns," Jimmy said, nodding in Jane's direction.

Jane, by now, had stopped at the base of one of the old oak trees which overlooked Jimmy's garden and the lane. The tree was a couple of centuries old. Its trunk was enormously wide and the tree towered over both man and property. A rope swing dangled from one of the sturdy branches over the lane below. Although the branch from which the rope was dangling, didn't hang over Jimmy's garden, some of the tree's branches did. The branches concerned were high up, true enough. If someone wanted to use them to jump into the garden it would involve some very daring acrobatics and a big drop to the ground, but it would be possible. Jane stared up at the tree and recalled a conversation she'd had with her husband a few weeks earlier, when he'd chanced to remark: "I used to love fence jumping when I was a boy."

It had been early evening, and they'd been sitting in their front room, Hugh hidden behind the newspaper and Jane taking up the hem of Adele's school pinafore. She'd looked at her husband, "And what, pray, is fence jumping, if I may be so bold as to ask?"

"It's like hurdling, only it's over fences," he'd explained patiently, looking up from his newspaper. "It says in the paper that a boy from Adele's school has just broken one of his legs fence jumping."

"I heard a boy had broken his leg. I wasn't aware of the full circumstances. I think he's a couple of years older than Adele. I believe he's now back at school, wearing a cast and relishing the attention, busily collecting signatures."

"The paper is getting quite worked up about it, suggesting fences should be made higher to stop it happening. How ridiculous," he'd said, getting quite worked up himself. "When I was a youngster, there was nothing me and my friends liked better than a spot of fence jumping. It was the challenge of getting over in one, that we used to love. The important thing is to be able to get a good run at it. It's essential, if you're to be able get over, or not as the case may be. Believe it or not, I was something of a rebel when I was young," he'd said with a grin.

Jane had returned to her needlework once more, only to be interrupted by her husband again.

"What I enjoyed even more than fence jumping was branch traversing. Shall I tell you what that is?"

"Please do. As if I can't guess."

"First you have to find your tree. The taller the better. Next you climb your tree, getting as high as you dare to. Remember, there are other boys watching and reputations are at stake.

Once you've selected your branch – it has to be as thick as you can find, but not too thick, it has to be able to bend – you slowly swing your way along the branch, swing – not walk, not crawl – swing. We're not talking about a tightrope walk here, you understand? No. We're a talking about swinging along a branch, holding on to it for dear life with both hands. The branch inevitably bends under the weight of the boy dangling down from it, allowing him to let go and drop gently onto the ground, if it doesn't break under his weight first, which is how my cousin came to break his arm. It's got to be high enough for there to be a challenge, but not so high that an accident is inevitable. Tall trees and high fences are too much of a challenge for any young boy to resist. Any attempt to stop it will just make things worse," he said, slapping the newspaper with the back of his hand to emphasise that this was a subject he felt quite strongly about.

Jane continued to stare up at the oak tree on the lane at the back of old Jimmy's garden. "Now I see how. I just need to know who and why? And to know that, all we need do is to catch your thieves red-handed," she said.

The plan was a simple one. They would lay a trap. Jimmy was to stand behind his stall selling his wares, whilst Jane would hide behind the old chicken coop and keep watch. Nothing happened for the first two afternoons. But on the third day, the thieves struck.

By this time, Jane had moved location and was sitting inside the garden shed, looking out over the garden through a peephole Jimmy had drilled in the wall of the shed especially for this purpose. Jane suspected that the thieves were likely to strike at any moment, because there were three large cauliflowers in the garden ready for picking. "It won't be long now, Jimmy," she said. "They won't be able to resist."

The rustling of leaves first alerted Jane to the thieves' presence. She focused her binoculars on the oak. After a few moments, she saw a young lad climbing up the tree trunk. Jane recognised him. It was one of the Russell twins, Colin and Clive, a pair of identical eleven-year-old twin boys who lived near her. Jane wasn't sure which one she was watching. Whichever one it was, she knew his brother wouldn't be far away. She watched as the boy reached a branch which overhung Jimmy's garden. He crawled along it for a very short distance, then took hold of the branch with both hands and began to slowly inch his way along it, crossing one arm over the other, his feet dangling below. The further he moved along the branch, the more it bent under his weight. Jane wondered if the branch might snap and the boy receive a painful comeuppance, but it wasn't to be. He was by now two thirds of the way along the branch. The branch had bent sufficiently low under his weight for him to be able to safely let go and fall to the ground. He landed on both feet. His legs bent under him and he fell over. It didn't take him long to jump to his feet. He quickly looked around and realising the coast was clear, he ran over to the vegetable patch. He took a pen knife out of his pocket and helped himself to both cauliflowers. With a cauliflower under each arm, he walked back up the garden towards the bungalow. From there he started to sprint along the garden. Still clutching the vegetables under his arms, he hurdled over the rear fence, one leg outstretched in front of the other. He cleared it in one and avoided stepping in the sand.

Jane could only laugh at his audacity. Once in, and crime committed, climbing over the back fence would have been an easier way to have made a fast exit, but it would have meant leaving footprints behind as evidence. Also, for a high-spirited young lad, climbing over a fence was nothing like as much fun as jumping over a fence. The boy's brother, Jane presumed, was somewhere out front, keeping watch. They had probably devised a simple warning cry, such as a loud whistle, for example.

Jane and Jimmy arrived at the home of the Russell twins some ten minutes later. They found the two boys playing football in a field to the rear of their back garden, one protecting a goal made from two jumpers placed on the ground, the other facing the goal, ready to take aim at a cauliflower on the ground in front of him, substituting as a football.

"Good Lord!" Jane said.

"Why don't you get your dad to buy you a real football?" Jimmy hollered at the boys. "'Stead of practicing your shots using my cauliflowers?"

They froze. The pitch was already covered with the remnants of the cauliflower they'd kicked from one end of the pitch to the other. Its florets and broken stalks were strewn over the field. The twins looked at each other. They wanted to scarper, but realised there wasn't any point as they were known to their victim by name.

"Someone confiscated our last football, and the one before that," one of the boys said.

"Got sick of you kicking it into his garden, did he?" Jimmy said.

"Through his window more like," the other one admitted.

The boys slouched over to join Jane and Jimmy at the side of the field.

"Our dad won't let us have another ball until we pay him back for the window," one of the two boys said.

"So you thought you'd help yourself to my cabbages and cauliflowers instead, did you?" Jimmy said, attempting to sound stern.

"We couldn't resist it," the other boy said. "Please don't tell our dad, old Jimmy. We won't have no pocket money left!"

"Which one are you?" Jimmy asked.

"Colin," the boy admitted.

"Well, Colin, I will tell your dad if you call me old again," Jimmy said.

"Sorry," the boy apologised.

"Tell you what. I won't tell on you, if you run some chores for me now and then and help me out when I ask you to," Jimmy said.

The boys both nodded quickly and eagerly.

"There's plenty needs doing both inside and outside. There's windows to wash and a drive to weed for a start."

"Anything, just don't grass us up," Clive said, with his brother nodding earnestly beside him.

"In exchange for which I'll let you use my football. It's made from real leather, you know."

"Thanks Jimmy, you're a good 'un," Colin said.

Clive ran back and retrieved the cauliflower from the ground, and returned with it, holding it out to the old man, who shook his head.

"See if you can score a penalty with it, lad," he said to Clive. "And you see if you can stop him," he said to Colin.

"Really?" they both asked.

"Really!" Jane said.

"Why not? I always plant too many, and besides, I haven't had much to laugh about since my missus passed over."

The boys quickly returned to the pitch. Watched by Jane and Jimmy, Clive took his position as goalie and Colin as striker. Colin carefully positioned the cauliflower on the ground, took a run at it, and with one massive kick sent the cauliflower flying over the head and outstretched arms of the goalie. It hit the ground, breaking in two.

"Goal," Colin yelled, jumping up and down and punching the air in triumph.

Jane and Jimmy returned to his bungalow.

"Jimmy, you're not really going to allow those two to clean the house are you? They'll never do it properly, you know. They'll make more of a mess than there already is, if you don't mind me saying so."

Jimmy turned to scowl at her.

"I was rather hoping you'd let me clean the bungalow for you. I do so love cleaning," she continued. "I find it cathartic. I get a real sense of satisfaction from seeing a job well done. I love to see everything gleaming. But Hugh is so tidy. He even clears up after Adele. I barely have anything left to do."

"You're just like my missus, you are."

"Why thank you Jimmy," Jane said, genuinely flattered by the compliment.

III

Jane's attention turned from her reminiscing, to the purchase of her new Smartphone and she continued on her way to the phone shop which was owned by the adult Colin Russell.

When she reached it, she found a crime scene waiting for her. Colin's seven-year-old son Kieran, guiltily peered out from behind his dad's legs, clutching a football for dear life, while his father apologised profusely to the owner of a car whose front windscreen was cracked from side to side. The crack emanated from a muddy football-shaped imprint in the middle of the windscreen. It didn't need a private detective to solve this one, Jane thought, suppressing a smile. Colin pressed money into the motorist's hands and apologised once again.

Once the motorist had driven away, Colin took his young son by his shoulders. "How many times have I told you not to kick your football into the road," he said.

"It wasn't my fault," the boy argued. "The car didn't come round the corner until I'd kicked it."

Colin was clearly about to argue further with his son when he spotted Jane. She greeted him with a wide smile. Colin looked down on his son, and ruffled his hair. "Don't do it again."

The rather surprised child stared at his dad for a few moments before saying, "No fear, dad."

After watching his son run away as fast as he could, Colin asked, "How can I help you, Jane?"

"I believe it's time I bought a Smartphone, Colin. I need it for my detective agency."

The two turned and walked into his shop.

"Jimmy Anderson's old place is back on the market, I see," Jane said, still trying to stop herself from laughing out loud.

"So I heard."

"Your lad seems to be a chip off the old block, or should I say young block," she said to Colin.

He opened a glass cabinet containing his range of phones and removed a selection of them. "Tell me about it," he said grimacing.

He placed the phones he'd taken from the cabinet on top of the counter.

"I made a list of all the things I need the phone to do," Jane said, handing Colin the list in question. She'd spent some time compiling it, adding something else when she thought of it. He glanced down the 'must-have' list:

take photos

internet

memos

maps

something I could use to kill time when staking out suspects.

Colin gave her an old-fashioned look and said, "You can't get a Smartphone that doesn't do all those things nowadays. You want a phone with maps, I can give you a phone with GPS tracking. Not sure where you are, I can give you a phone that can hazard a guess."

"Really?" she said.

"Really," he replied. "We've got camera phones, music phones, fashion phones, gaming phones, phones for social climbers, phones for social networkers, phones for those too young to social network but who do anyway. They're usually bright pink and called Best Mate. We've got phones to help you organise your life, entertain you and impress people with how organised, entertaining and impressive you are. The only phones we don't have are phones for antisocial recluses, 'cos they don't use 'em."

Jane stared at the selection in front of her.

"Please choose the one you think most suitable," she said.

Colin pushed one in her direction. She quite liked the look of it. It was curved and made from chrome.

"It'll do everything you want and more. You'll see it's better turned out and a bit more curvaceous than some of the others," he said. "Not unlike yourself, Jane."

"I'll take it."

Some minutes passed while Colin set up Jane's new Smartphone for her with her existing telephone number and e-mail address. When he finished, he said, "You have mail."

Jane realised she hadn't checked her e-mails since she'd left for Greenfields. She took the phone from him. The e-mail was from Charity. It was unusual for Charity to send her e-mails, with her living next door. She opened it to find the photos of Johnny's underwear shoot, but unlike everyone else who'd received the photographs of Johnny in his thong, she did not scream with laughter. She did not think the photographs funny. Even Colin's wry comments – "Think my missus would like to meet him!" – couldn't force a smile. Her only response to these photographs was to think – Now I remember where I've seen you before, Monty!

CHAPTER TWENTY-SEVEN

Mantrap

I

Monty was the man who'd climbed the tentpole at the bikers' rally. No wonder she hadn't immediately recognised him. She'd been trying to look anywhere but at him. Monty didn't know Pete Lambert. He was a show-off and a chancer who'd do anything to entertain an audience, and if he could earn himself a bit of money from it then so much the better.

She had little doubt he was already busy entertaining all his friends at her expense with an amusing story about gullible old ladies. She sent him a text asking how his search for Peter Lambert was going and got a quick response.

'He's been spotted in a betting shop. I'm on his trail! Can you send me more money? I'll need it if I'm to track him down!'

She turned her phone off. She could have screamed in frustration. Not because of the lost money or time, but because she was no further forward in finding Pete Lambert than she had been at the beginning of the month. She was really not in a good mood by the time she got home.

"What that Monty needs is a visit from the police," she told Maria.

"You should call them," Maria said, handing her a freshly made coffee, and sitting down beside her at the kitchen table.

"I don't know what I'm going to do Maria, I'm not getting anywhere in my search for Johnny's father, and I still have no idea where the young girl I followed has come by so much money. It's so frustrating. I know I said I wanted a challenge, but this is getting ridiculous!"

"I confident you will solve all your cases soon," Maria said with a knowing smile.

"I'm glad one of us is."

"I have a special reason for confidence."

"Which is?"

"You remember I also clean for witch, yes?"

"I do remember," Jane said, wondering why Maria was raising this now. "A white witch I believe."

"Very white. She only go out if full moon. I tell her of you only yesterday. I say you very clever lady, but sometimes even you are ..." she struggled to find the English word.

"Stumped?" Jane suggested.

"Yes, stumped. I tell her this and she say we must straight away cast spell for the unstumping."

"Cast a spell for the what?"

"She has a spell for everything. You name it, she casts it. So we do. We make magick for you. We cast for you spell of inspiration." Maria said.

Jane did not know whether to laugh or cry, or look for a new home help.

"You not believe?" Maria asked.

"Not really."

"Me, I have open mind. You should also. There more things in heaven and earth. Many people say so."

"So I understand."

"A spell of inspiration take twenty-four hours to work. We make twenty-four hours ago. That means any minute now it will take effect."

At that moment, Jane's phone rang. It was Stella Barnes.

"I'm actually in the middle of my ironing…" Stella said "…but I had to stop to call you straight away. I've suddenly remembered something Pete did years ago. It's just come to me out of the blue. My youngest's really into the band Franks. I don't know if you've heard of them, but you would have if you were a teenage boy."

Jane said she hadn't.

"You haven't missed much. Like I said, he's really into them. Every single one of his T-shirts have the name Franks on them it. Must have been ironing the same logo twenty times which jogged my memory. When Pete was about fifteen, he was busted by the police for joyriding. He got out of it by giving the police a false name and address."

"Can you remember the name?"

"That's just it. I can. The name he gave to the police was Franks. Johnny Franks. It was the name of the place he played snooker in. It was actually called the Sir James Frank Hall, but everyone called it Johnny Franks. He said the name just came into his head. I don't know if it helps?"

This information lifted Jane's spirit enormously. The clue provided by Stella Barnes may prove to be another red herring but at least it gave her something to go on. She said the same to Stella.

"Let me know if you track the weasel down, won't you?"

"I will, Stella."

Jane replaced the receiver. She caught Maria watching her, clearly having overheard the whole call. The smirk she wore said, told you. Jane ignored her and went to her study.

Her internet search for Johnny Franks revealed some entries. Jane quickly scanned down the list. She didn't think any of them were her man – they were either too young or the wrong nationality to be Johnny's father. She leaned back in her chair and thought for a few moments. She typed in 'Dockworkers + Franks' but this didn't bring up any entries. Not another dead end, she thought, but then she had an idea. From the desk drawer she took out the Blackpool postcard and looked at it again. She turned it over. *An Amusement Park, Blackpool* was the card's only description of the photograph on it. She studied the photograph again. She could see the letters LL'S in the background. She knew it had been taken twenty-six years earlier. Jane, what an idiot you have been, she thought typing, Amusement Parks, Blackpool, and the decade in question.

A number of entries appeared, the first of which related to a Howell's Amusement Park in Blackpool. She opened the entry but didn't need to read it because a photograph of its wrought iron entrance gates, with the name Howell's emblazoned across them, told her this was where the photograph had been taken.

The name rang a bell. She quickly typed, 'Dockworkers + Howells'. The fourth entry on the list was the one she wanted. It related to the secretary of the North Eastern branch of the Retired Dockworkers' Association – Tom Howells. She'd read the entry before but hadn't made the connection.

Jane clicked on the link to the Association's secretary. This bought up a bio of Tom Howells, but unfortunately no photograph. Jane read on and learnt that as a reward for his tireless efforts on behalf of retired, disabled or deceased dockworkers and their families, Tom Howells had been unanimously elected as the secretary general of the Newcastle and North Eastern branch of the RDA for the tenth year running.

Did she have her man, she wondered? Tom Howells was a retired dockworker and probably about the right age. How could she establish for definite he was Johnny's father though? E-mail was no good – she'd have to visit Newcastle and speak to him face-to-face, but if he denied it flat out, then what?

She looked out onto her garden and over to her summer-house, where she had spent most of the last month setting traps. This gave her an idea. If she could set a trap to catch a mouse, she must be able to set a trap to catch Tom Howells. And not just one to catch him, but one which would tell her, one way or the other, whether Pete Lambert and Tom Howells were one in the same. Only what? She watched as Charity's cat, Addison, crossed her lawn. Like her, Addison was hunting. A plan started to form in her mind.

II

Jane, Miles Dawson-Jones and his mother Mirabella, gathered around the hearth of the rectory's drawing-room, warmed by a roaring wood fire. Mirabella poured the tea, while Jane explained what she wanted and why.

"I need help in setting a trap, and knowing how good you are on the computer Miles, I wondered if you could help. I need someone to prepare a poster for me, purporting offering a prize, with which to lure someone out of his lair." Jane explained in more detail the nature of the trap she wished to set, "Remembering Johnny and Jack trying to trap my harvest mouse with an old game of *Mousetrap* gave me the idea," she said. "We'll need a webpage so he can get in touch."

III

Miles and Mirabella called at Jane's cottage the very next day, with Miles clutching a laptop. Jane showed them into the living room.

"I had fun doing this," Miles said of the poster and webpage he'd prepared.

"Before we start," Jane said, "let me pour everyone a drink."

She returned from the kitchen moments later holding a tray on which stood a gin and tonic for Mirabella and herself, and even though he wasn't quite old enough to drink alcohol, a bottle of stout for Miles, half of which she'd poured into a pint glass. She placed both bottle and glass on the table next to him, with the words, "Don't tell your mother."

Miles opened the laptop to show Jane the poster he'd designed. The postcard featuring Johnny's father as *Tom* appeared above the words:-

To celebrate the launch of our exciting new game of cat and mouse CAT-TRAP!

we're looking for the Tom in this postcard. Is it you? If you think it is, please let us know and a holiday for two will be yours.

Proof of identity will be required before the winner is declared.

198

Part of a CAT-TRAP! promotional offer.
www.cat-trap@cat-trap.com

Jane thought the fake webpage Miles showed her next, even better than the poster. He'd based it on the home page of a well-known toy manufacturer. It featured a team of mice wearing army fatigues, trying to drop a giant tin of cat food over a sleeping cat, who suddenly sprang into life, his claws opening into an arsenal of weaponry, scattering the mice in every direction, and the caption:-

See if you can catch Tom – but remember this cat is a light sleeper and if you wake him up – you're cat food!

Available as both a board game and online-gaming.

Miles had even added a Contact Us address, and the game's purported release date. A link led to The *Tom and Jerry* poster, and a tantalising promise of more promotional offers to come.

"Miles, you've excelled yourself," Jane said.

"I told him he should copyright it," his mother said, "it looks such fun."

"I only hope it works," Jane replied. "It will entail a visit to Newcastle to put the posters up near the Dockworker's Association, and possibly another one if he sees them and gets in touch. But my time is nothing if it helps Johnny put his demons to rest."

CHAPTER TWENTY-EIGHT

Jane Sets Her Trap

Jane travelled to Newcastle by train, taking the scenic East Coast route along the coastline. She left Southstoft by the first train, and arrived by afternoon, taking a taxi straight to the Newcastle branch of the Retired Dockworkers' Association. This turned out to be on the ground floor of a Working Man's Club. Jane wasn't sure they'd allow her poster to be displayed (a bit capitalist, she thought) but there was no harm in asking.

The hallway of the Working Man's Club couldn't have been redecorated at any time during the last forty plus years. Its khaki curtains were thread bare, its walls covered in cheap wooden panelling under hound-tooth-patterned wall paper, paint peeled from the iron stairwell running up the middle of the wide double staircase, the ceiling was nicotine stained and what purported to be the club's official notice board was no more than gold letters stuck onto green felt. Swing doors, to the right of the stairs, led to the club's bar. Jane pushed open the doors and found herself in a large dingy room, laid out with tables, where a solitary barmaid was setting up for the evening.

Jane showed the barmaid the poster, explaining that she was employed by the toy company to find places to display the posters, in exchange for which, she had authority to pay a small fee. This seemed to do the trick, and she left with a poster displayed on the bar's wall.

A 'greasy spoon' type cafe serving all-day English breakfasts, called the Butterfly Cafe, adjoined the Working Man's Club. The cafe's nameplate touched the nameplate of the Working Man's Club, causing some wag to take it upon himself to cross out the words, The Butterfly Cafe, and write in its place The Gentleman's Club. Jane thought it likely Johnny's father would visit the cafe given its proximity to his workplace. She peered through its window. At one table a man hungrily devoured a bacon sandwich, washed down by a mug of tea. At another, a group of gentlemen enjoyed full English breakfasts, despite it being late afternoon. Jane wondered if any of them could be Johnny's father. She walked through the doors and over to the counter where she repeated her story to the lady serving there. She turned out to be the cafe's owner and readily agreed to display a poster in the cafe's window for a small cash sum.

Jane left the cafe happy. She managed to get two posters displayed prominently in places likely to be frequented by Tom Howells/Pete Lambert.

Although she spent the remaining part of the day putting up posters wherever she could, including on the poster board of a nearby underpass and some lampposts, she knew that if Johnny's father responded, it would most likely be to the posters in the Working Man's Club or the Butterfly Cafe. By now it was early evening and growing dark and so she took a taxi to the hotel she'd booked for the night.

CHAPTER TWENTY-NINE

The Bait is Taken

The first thing Jane did after breakfast the next morning was check her messages. Unsurprisingly, given she'd only put the posters up late the day before, Tom Howells hadn't responded to the bait. She decided to remain in Newcastle for a few days in the hope that he would get in touch.

Her hotel overlooked the River Tyne. It was impossible for the eye not be drawn to the art gallery on the other side of the river. That it had once been a quayside grain warehouse was clear from its architecture. Lest there be any doubt, the words Baltic Flour Mill remained carved on the front of the building in enormous black capital lettering. Enormous banners advertised an exhibition by Adelaide Kincaid. Adelaide Kincaid was an artist who was about the same age as Jane. Her cartoon-like paintings of ordinary people behaving outlandishly always made Jane laugh, however miserable she was feeling, just as Stanley Marshman's poem's did. Knowing she would spend a very enjoyable morning at the art gallery, she made her way there, stopping briefly on the quayside to admire the very modern bridge (two curved steel arches, supported by suspension cables, creating a near-perfect semicircle) she was about to cross.

Jane stared along the river. Although a cargo boat sailed towards the bridge, unfortunately it wasn't large enough to warrant the bridge opening – something Jane understood to be a spectacular sight – and she carried on.

The bridge was busy. When half-way across it she decided to sit down and people watch, one of her favourite occupations. Two Muslim women swathed in their traditional burkas passed her at the same time as two other young women, defying the cold in their miniskirts and short cropped tops, crossed in the opposite direction. One had a chain looped through her bellybutton, the other a tattoo covering most of her lower back, although Jane couldn't be sure what of.

A young woman pushing a pushbike on the cycle path below caught Jane's eye. The cyclist stopped a short way from Jane, and seemingly transfixed by something on the bridge, started to push her bike backwards and forwards. Jane leant forward to establish what she was targeting. She was left feeling rather disconcerted when she realised the girl was deliberately squashing some unfortunate flying ants under the wheels of her bike. Two other girls, sitting nearby, squealed in disgust when they too realised what she was doing. Jane heard one of them say to the other, "I'm a bit Buddhist, about stuff like that." The ant-killing girl appeared oblivious to the effect she was having on her audience, and seemed determined to carry on crushing innocent insects under the wheels of her bike until all were annihilated. Jane felt it was time for her to move, however, no sooner had she stood up than her phone buzzed to tell her she'd received an e-mail. She studied the screen. To her astonishment, Tom Howells had sent an e-mail to the Cat -Trap website. She moved to another bench (so as not to be distracted by ant-girl) and read the message.

'I'm your man! The one in the postcard!' it began. 'I'm the one playing Tom. Don't know how that became public. Boy, that must have been taken nigh on twenty-eight years ago. I was working there at the time – on the dodgems. I can send you other photos of me taken at the same time. I've got another one of me as Jerry, if you want to see it, as proof like…'

The message rambled on, but Jane didn't read any more. She sent him a holding e-mail, purportedly from the toy company which Miles had prepared, acknowledging receipt of Tom Howells' e-mail and promising a call from a representative within the next few days. She had an e-mail of her own to send Tom Howells – one she'd prepared before she left Failsham – but contacting him immediately might raise his suspicions. She'd go to the gallery first.

Well, well, well, Jane thought, as she crossed the bridge, in only a few hours she might finally meet Johnny Lambert's father.

Jane spent the next few hours at the exhibition, and found herself smiling at almost every painting she stopped to look at. She ended her visit by purchasing a couple of brightly coloured Adelaide Kincaid prints in the gallery's shop. Both were typical of the artist. In the first print, a very large young lady tried to squeeze herself into a pair of stiletto shoes, clearly at least a size too small for her feet. In the second, an elderly couple, grey-haired and stooping, hobbled down a street arm-in-arm. The old man ogled a poster of a skimpily dressed young lady on to a nearby advertising hoarding, whilst his wife ogled a life-size cardboard cut-out of a good-looking young man, dressed in Bermuda shorts, displayed in a shop window. Jane decided to send the first print to her daughter as a present, and keep the other herself.

From the gallery's restaurant she sent Tom Howells her e-mail. She used her own e-mail address and sent it to the contact details given as his on the Dockworkers' Association webpage.

'Dear Mr Howells,

My grandfather was a docker on the London docks during the 1920s. He perished after falling from scaffolding where he'd been working without a safety harness, something which was all too common in those days. I've been doing a great deal of online research and have come across your name. I'm interested in learning more about the lives of the men who work on the docks, and I wondered, as you clearly have first-hand knowledge, if we might meet up? I'm in Newcastle this afternoon, if that's any good for you?

Mrs Jane Hetherington.'

Everything in the e-mail was pretty much true, up to a point. Whilst Jane was interested in learning more about the lives of the men who worked on the docks alongside her grandfather, she wasn't interested in learning it from Pete Lambert/Tom Howells. Nonetheless, Jane had no hesitation in sending the e-mail. If Tom Howells was really Johnny's father then he clearly played by a different set of rules to other people and honesty didn't appear to be amongst those rules.

She received a reply by return.

'I'd be delighted to meet you whenever you'd like. I'm around all today.

Tom Howells.'

She replied immediately. 'Two o'clock this afternoon?'

'See you then -- T. H.'

206

CHAPTER THIRTY

Pete Lambert

Jane arrived at the Working Man's Club where Tom Howells had his office in good time for their meeting, only to learn that he was running late. She suspected he was one of a group of men she'd just passed standing outside smoking. Hopefully this would put him in a relaxed state of mind.

"If I ever feel like taking up smoking again I'll just come here and inhale instead," Jane joked with the young man escorting her to the waiting room. Despite the smoking ban, years of heavy smoking in the Working Man's Club had left its indelible mark.

"You what?" he said.

"Nothing."

Jane followed him down the hallway to the small reception room, where she was instructed to wait until Mr Howells arrived. The waiting room had nothing more in it than a few hard plastic chairs and a table. Jane picked up the only magazine there - *the Socialist Worker*- and flicked through it. She hadn't realised it was still going.

Her sister Jill, rebelling against her petty, middle-class, bourgeoisie upbringing (as she'd put it) had joined the

Communist Party the day she turned seventeen, something their more-amused-than-bemused parents had thought no more than a phase. Jill once dragged Jane to a meeting of her local Communist Party branch. Not before, nor since, had Jane seen so many people smoke so many cigarettes filled with so many different substances in such a confined space. Nor had she ever heard the words Dialectic Materialism and Capitalistic Imperialism (could Stan use these words in a poem, she now wondered) spoken so many times, or indeed at all. The evening had ended with Jane desperately attempting to keep a straight face, whilst everyone else in the room, including her sister, got to their feet to give an earnest rendition of the Red Flag, each with their eyes closed, heads bowed, and right fists raised in the air.

Jane's parents had always blamed the people in that room for their daughter's early death. Jill's boyfriend, whose reckless motorcycle driving at high speed whilst high on marijuana caused both of their deaths, had been a member of the Communist Party, and through him Jane's sister converted to the cause. But Jane did not blame him, nor anyone else for what happened to her sister. Jill had been born with a death wish, and that was all that was to it.

"It's my destiny to die young!" the beautiful Jill had often said, twirling around the bedroom the girls shared. "I love to dice with death, otherwise why be alive?"

Jane knew she couldn't start crying again. She had to focus on the job in hand. She put down the magazine and took out the photograph of Johnny's father. She propped it up in her handbag in a position where she could surreptitiously compare it with the Tom Howells she was about to meet.

208

He arrived moments later. He did not look a well man. He was out of breath and had to stop to puff at an inhaler before he could even shake her hand.

While they were still in the waiting room, she stared at the photograph in her bag, then back at him. There seemed little doubt that they were one and the same person. The man in the photograph given to her by Johnny was a younger, slimmer version of the heavier, older man in front of her. The features were the same in both: the eyes, small and dark; the eyebrows, bushy and black; and the nose which looked as though it had once been broken. His hair hadn't receded very much, and in many ways, Jane could see a resemblance to Johnny more in the later photograph than the earlier one.

Tom Howells showed Jane into his office, but even as he sat down at his desk, he needed a second puff at his inhaler. His office looked out on to a narrow street at the back of the building. It was quite large, but cluttered with files, boxes of paperwork and piles of books. From what Jane could see, each one was a good worthy Socialist tract. Tom Howells sat behind his large desk and Jane sat across it from him.

"Emphysema," he explained, following yet another puff of the inhaler.

He continually played with an empty ashtray on his desk, running his fingers round the rim. Now that Jane was face to face with Johnny Lamberts' father, she could see he looked a good deal older than his sixty years.

"So your granddad was on the docks, was he?" Tom wheezed as he spoke.

"Greenwich," she replied truthfully. "He died falling from scaffolding. Someone died on those docks every week in those days. No one can believe it nowadays, in our health and safety conscious world."

"Working men still die in preventable industrial accidents all the time, Mrs Hetherington. And from industrial diseases, myself being a case in question," he said, leaning across his desk and pointing at her, to make his point. "People think health and safety has put a stop to all of this, but it hasn't," he wheezed angrily. He would have continued, but breathlessness forced him to stop. He puffed on his inhaler three more times. "It's vital that people understand the hardship still suffered by the working man up and down the country."

Whilst Jane did not entirely disagree with the sentiments, this topic was getting her nowhere. She had no alternative but to interrupt him and steer the subject matter around to the reason for her visit. "Do you have a son who works on the docks?" she asked.

"I don't have a son at all," he replied brazenly. "I don't have any kids as a matter of fact. I've had three wives and now I don't have one. No more women for me."

"Actually I think you do have a son, Mr Howells, or should I call you Mr Lambert? You have a son called Johnny."

He stared at her. He was speechless. Too shocked even to reach for his inhaler.

"Sue?" he finally managed to gasp.

"You flatter me," Jane said, for her neighbour's mother would have been a decade younger than she.

"My name really is Jane Hetherington and although I did have a grandfather who died on the docks, this is not the reason for my visit to you today. You see, I live next door to your son, Johnny. He asked me to try and find you. I'm a private detective. You turned out to be very elusive, Tom, or should I say Pete? It was a job to find you, but as you can see I did, and so here I am. And rather more to the point, here you are."

"My God!" Another puff at the inhaler followed. "I haven't thought about him and his mum since the day I left. This is too much, I need a fag."

He opened the drawer of his desk and pulled out a packet of cigarettes. "I know, I know, smoking indoors is illegal, but they can't shoot me for it, can they?"

He lit up a cigarette and began to smoke it. This made him cough. Even so, he continued to smoke, though every breath was clearly agony for him. Jane used to smoke. As she knew only too well, smoking was every smoker's closest friend to whom one could always return in one's hour of need, even after a decade's absence. Eventually, he held out the packet to Jane. She was so annoyed she almost took one, but remembering how long it had taken her to give up, declined his offer.

He continued to smoke, unable even to look at her. This moment was not something he had ever thought would happen to him, and he'd made no preparations for it. He had no way of dealing with it, other than to hide behind a mask of cigarette smoke.

"I think I should tell you that your son is alive and well. However, his mother died a few years ago."

"Sue's dead? I didn't know that."

Well, you wouldn't, would you, Jane thought crossly.

"She have any more kids?"

"She didn't remarry, nor have any more children, that I'm aware of."

"Thought she would," he said, awkwardly.

"Well she didn't," Jane snapped, inadvertently allowing herself to sound as angry as she felt.

"We weren't getting on, you see. Thought it best if I left. Make a fresh start, like. I'll be honest. I put her and the kiddie right out of me mind like. I closed that door behind me. Thought she'd do the same thing."

Jane made no comment.

"He's well, you say, my boy?"

Jane nodded and said, "As is your half-sister Stella, although she's Stella Barnes now."

Another silence followed this revelation. This allowed Jane to scrutinise Tom Howells carefully. He put out his cigarette and played with the cigarette lighter, twisting it around his fingers. With his head half-bowed and still avoiding eye contact, he mulled over the news. Jane had never been able to understand how some people were able to disassociate themselves from the enormity of their actions; nor the ease with which some were able to convince themselves that their actions were for the best, even when they were plainly cruel and selfish. Pete Lambert was a case in hand. He'd wiped the existence of his first wife and son from his memory without a qualm, and persuaded himself that because he'd moved on with his life without a thought for the past, so would Sue and Johnny. It simply hadn't occurred to him that for those rejected, moving on was not so easy. Jane had no idea whether the embarrassment and awkwardness he was displaying, reflected real sorrow and remorse for his actions from years ago, or not.

"Stella got your letter," Jane said. "She went to the Fleet and waited for you there. She even went back the next month. Did you change your mind?"

212

When Tom Howells looked completely blank, Jane said, "You sent Stella a letter asking that she met you in the Fleet, in Gore…"

"I never did! I haven't been near the Fleet since I married Sue."

"It was a long time ago."

"I never did, I tell you. I put the whole lot of them out of my mind when I went."

"You sent Sue a postcard from Blackpool. I used it to find you – I'm Cat-Trap by the way. You haven't won a holiday I'm afraid."

He stared at her for a few moments then said, "I didn't send the card no more than I sent a letter. I don't know who sent the letter, but I know the lady in the photograph sent the card to Sue. I made the mistake of telling her about Sue. She said she did it so's Sue'd know to get on with her life. Not sure I believe that. I knew Sue would use it to find me, so I changed my name again to something I knew I could remember, and moved on again without either of them."

An uneasy silence followed.

"Could you tell my boy something for me?" he eventually said.

CHAPTER THIRTY-ONE

The Olive Branch

Johnny felt rather pleased with himself. He'd earned good money lobbing a tree on the common. He slammed the money onto the kitchen table. "Not bad for a day's work, eh?" he said. "I've finally got enough to take you skiing. Where and when do you want to go – St. Moritz!"

When Charity didn't reply, he said, "Look a bit happier about it, won't you? I've worked my what-sits off to take you skiing. I know, I know – it's the least I can do after what I did, etc, etc – but I am trying to make amends here."

"Johnny," a sombre sounding Charity said, "Jane's here. She's got something to tell you."

The couple moved to join Jane in the front room, where she told Johnny about her meeting with his father that morning. She left nothing out, nor did she embellish anything. She merely informed Johnny factually how she'd tracked down his father and then she repeated the conversation she'd had with him.

"So he's dying then?" Charity said. If her words sounded harsh, it was because they were said without a shred of sympathy, for she felt none.

"I'm afraid that if you wish to make peace with your father, Johnny, you must do it now," Jane said softly.

At that moment, Jack walked into the room. Responding to the silence, he asked, "Why are you lot so quiet? What's going on?"

"Jane's found me old man," Johnny said.

"Told you she was good," Jack said, disappearing out of the room again.

Jane rose. "I'm sure you two have a lot to talk about. I'll leave you alone. I'll show myself out."

Jane followed Jack into the kitchen. She found him leaning up against one of the kitchen units, hungrily eating a bag of cheese and onion crisps.

"Wonder what Johnny'll do?" Jack mused. "Dunno what I'd do if I was him. It's not right what his dad did. Not sure I'd want to see him again if I was Johnny."

Jane wasn't either. To change the subject, she pointed to the words emblazoned across to the bag of crisps:-

'Is there £100,000 inside this packet?!?'

"I presume there wasn't?"

Jack glanced at the packet. "Na. Someone's already won it, worst luck. They claimed the prize months ago. I couldn't believe it when I heard. You wouldn't believe how many bags of crisps me, Johnny and Charity have eaten, and all we ever seem to get are these."

He reached behind him, and from a bowl on the worktop, picked up the same 'prize' Felix had won with his crisps – the picture of a man spread-eagled against a brick wall and the words:- Better Luck Next Time!

"We haven't even won so much as a free bag of crisps, let alone one hundred thousand pounds. It sucks," Jack said.

As Jane stared at the tiny picture, an idea hit her like the brick wall in the picture. Wasn't it Oscar Wilde who said he could resist anything but temptation?

Jack tipped the remains of the bag of crisps into his mouth to finish them off, and made to throw the empty crisp bag in the bin.

"Could I?" Jane asked.

Jack handed it to her. She flattened out the empty bag and stared at it.

"You don't happen to know who won the one hundred thousand pounds do you?" she asked him. "Was it a man or a woman? Someone young or old?"

"It was an eighteen year old girl. When Charity heard, she said: 'The money won't make her happy,' and I said, 'bet it will'."

"I don't think it has," Jane said, still staring at the crisp bag in her hand.

"You know who won it?"

"I think I might."

"Who?"

"A young woman called Lucy."

She wondered why she hadn't worked it out the moment Felix had stood up at the bikers' rally with a raffle ticket which didn't really belong to him, trying to claim a prize which wasn't his.

Jane quickly returned home to set another trap. With her own number withheld, and her new Smartphone set to 'record', she telephoned Lucy Erpingham. She introduced herself, using her maiden name.

"My name is Jane Preston, and I represent the Frazer Crisps' promotional department. I understand that you recently claimed the one hundred thousand pounds cash prize?"

"Er, er..."

"There is no easy way for me to put this, and on behalf of my company I must apologise profusely, but I'm afraid we're going to have to ask you for it back."

"What?" Lucy shrieked. "You can't. You can't."

"I'm afraid someone else is maintaining that the winning envelope in fact belonged to them, and the prize was claimed without their knowledge or agreement. We're going to have to verify who is the genuine winner, and why two winners have come forward. Let's not make this any more difficult than it already is."

"I'm the real winner," Lucy said. "I found the envelope. I showed you the receipt. The money is mine. Those other people are lying. They're...Oh my God!"

The line went dead at Lucy's end.

Jane immediately sent an e-mail to Jodie, with the telephone recording attached.

'I think I have established how your sister came across the money she's so gaily spending, and why she is avoiding you. However, I must warn you, you are not going to like what you're about to learn.'

CHAPTER THIRTY-TWO

Will No One Rid Me of this Turbulent Mouse?

The following morning, as Jane scattered seeds along the tree-lined border which separated her property from the field at its rear, an anxious looking Maria summoned her to the summerhouse. The look on Maria's face told Jane she was not to be confronted with good news.

"He's found his way back!" Maria said, pointing to the mouse droppings on the floor of the summerhouse.

"There's nothing for it but poison," Jane said wearily.

"Poison! You put him far away, yet he back already. The mouse must be genius to make such epic journey! He deserves our respect."

Jane thought this show of horror ironic, coming from a woman who was proposing death by a blunt instrument for the mouse only a few weeks earlier.

"It can't be the same mouse. I must have an infestation. I'll be overrun. I don't want to either, but what's the alternative?"

"Magick!" Maria said.

"Magick?"

"My white witch has magicked away hundreds of mouses – she's told me so. She says spells. Mouses leave. No lives lost."

Jane studied her to see whether or not she was joking. Apparently she wasn't.

"I think I need more than a sprinkling of fairy dust, Maria."

Maria, it seemed, was not going to give up without a fight. A bit like the mouse.

"Her magick help you before. Why not now?"

"When did it help me before?"

"You solve your cases only when we cast for you spell of inspiration. How else you explain?"

"I like to think I played some part, Maria," Jane murmured.

"You played your part after spell of inspiration inspire you," Maria said, now clearly a convert to Wicca. "Anyway, where harm in trying magick? You nice lady. You try not to hurt animals. As you say yourself, not many mouses like yours left in wild."

This was true, thought Jane. Not only that, but the mouse, or mice, had, in their own way, helped her track down Johnny's father.

"Well, I suppose it might be worth giving it a go. I'd rather not have to share my summerhouse with the carcasses of decaying mice, although I remain to be convinced."

Jane left Maria calling her white witch and returned to scattering her seeds. Johnny appeared in his back garden. She hadn't seen him since the evening before. She waved at him, and he jumped over the fence and walked over to join her.

"I bought these last year," she said. "I've never seen them before. They're a type of poppy. They like shade and woodland-like soil. I thought a few clumps along the border here would look nice." She poured some more seeds into her hand, then handed Johnny the packet to study.

Johnny read the packet. The flowers were called Stytophorum. They had bright yellow, saucer-shaped petals and wide lobed leaves. Judging by the picture, the leaves grew on long stalks to stand taller than the flowers. Jane was right, he thought – clumps of them spreading along the ground here would look nice. He poured some of the seeds into his own hand and threw them under the base of a tree.

"I've decided not to contact my father," he said.

Jane hurled the last of the seeds in her hand away into the distance.

"No?" she asked softly.

"Since he walked out, not a moment has gone by when I haven't thought about him, but he hasn't thought about me and Mum once. Not once. How could he think walking out wouldn't devastate me and Mum? Did he really think we'd just move on without a care in the world 'cos he could? He's my Dad. He was her husband. You care more about me than he does."

His words were spoken in such a tone of anguish and disappointment it broke Jane's heart to hear them. She did care about him, and so did Charity, and Jack and Stella. They all cared about him – deeply. She reached out and touched his arm. "Cup of tea?" she asked. "I still have some of those Garibaldi biscuits left, I think."

As the two walked back to the house together, Johnny said, "Don't know what I expected. Guess I hoped there was a nicer explanation, you know, like he wanted to come back but couldn't for some reason, or he had amnesia or something."

Once they were indoors, Jane filled the kettle while Johnny sat down at the kitchen table.

"I was lucky with my parents," she said. "So was Hugh, but his mother, Hettie wasn't. Her father was a heavy drinker. He once marooned her mother, brother and herself in London, when she was still just a child. They'd driven down as a family. Her mother had taken them shopping, whilst her father went to see one of his business partners. It must have been what's called a wet lunch, because he was so drunk afterwards that he drove back home without them. People didn't worry about drink driving then, it wasn't even illegal. Her poor mother had so little money on her, she had to beg the guard to let her and the children travel on the train without a ticket. Her father had to meet her at the station, and settle up with the guard. Married women didn't have their own credit cards back then." She placed the pot of tea and the biscuits on the table. "You know what they say – you can pick your friends, but you can't pick your family. Unfortunately, that's all too true." To lighten the mood, she said, "I hear you've raised enough for the holiday?"

"Yeah. Didn't need as much now Jack's not going."

"Is he not?"

"He wants to stay here, to be with Polly. He wants to stay at our place by himself, but Charity won't have it. Can he bunk down here for the week? Otherwise I think we'll all be staying."

"Of course he can. It'll be nice to have the company."

Johnny's phone began to ring.

"It's Felix," he said, answering it. "Hey Felix, how's it going?"

Felix hurriedly returned the greeting before launching into a rant: "Okay, let me start at the beginning. Last night I saw smoke rising from the churchyard and thinking a fire had broken out, Miles and I rushed over there, but when we got there all we found was a saucepan abandoned in a camp fire. Miles thought he heard someone say a name – Dee, Lee, Bee, Itmee – or something, but there was no one there. The pan had some vile sticky liquid in the bottom. I tasted it. It was cough mixture. I've found plenty of empty cough mixture bottles in churchyards over the years, but never some warmed up before! Anyway, I've had enough. I've bought one of those mosquito things which make an abominable shrieking noise, only audible to the under twenty-ones. I tested it on mine, it worked a treat. It drove them nuts!" he said, with a chuckle. "Personally I'd make them compulsory on all public buildings."

Although Johnny found Felix's rant quite enjoyable, he couldn't help wondering where he came in.

"In case you're wondering where you come in, I want someone to try it out, by loitering around the church yard with it concealed on their person. If it works, I'm having one fitted in the Belfry. In for it?"

"Seems you're not the only one with a vermin problem, Jane," Johnny said, when off the phone.

CHAPTER THIRTY-THREE

The Whine of the Mosquito

Johnny arrived at the churchyard at about ten in the evening with the Mosquito in his jacket pocket. It was deserted. He started with a nonchalant stroll around the graveyard, his hands in his jeans' pocket. He crossed the churchyard intending to walk through the wooden, thatched lych gate, and down the lych gate steps at the rear of the churchyard, which lead to a bridle path below.

When he reached the top of the gate, he saw a group of youngsters congregated at the bottom of the steps, clutching bottles of cider. He'd heard them complaining about the whine before he'd seen them. One of them said: "What the...!" and thrust his hands to his ears. The complaining and bewilderment as to the source of the ear piercing shriek, worsened as Johnny walked down the steps towards them. They instinctively moved away from the steps. Johnny nodded in their direction and walked towards them. Some in the group started swearing loudly, the whine clearly making the whole group feel very uncomfortable and disorientated. When Johnny bent down to do up an undone shoelace, someone said, "Let's get the hell out of here!" and the group slouched away.

Johnny turned right and walked along the bridle path which ran from behind Jane's cottage to the end of Rectory Road. At its end, he turned right into North Road, and from there took a sharp right into Rectory Road. He walked past the Rectory and back into the church, where he took another turn of the church yard. Next to visit it was a young couple. They must both have been over twenty-one, as they appeared more troubled by Johnny's unexpected presence than by any noise.

When they chanced upon him there, they immediately slowed their pace to a standstill. He knew they wanted him to leave them alone in the churchyard. He tried to keep a straight face as he leant against the church to light up a cigarette. He felt them look in his direction, but didn't return their gaze. The couple quickly left the churchyard.

A second group of youngsters turned up minutes later, only to turn on their heels and walk away quickly, moaning: 'What's that noise?' and 'It's doing my head in!'

Johnny hung around the graveyard for a while longer, but when no one else appeared, he walked down the steps again and back along the bridle path. He repeated the walk which returned him to the church. For the third time that evening he walked around it, but there was no one else in sight. He kept this up for some time, but word must have got around because no one else paid a visit to the churchyard while he was in it.

Rather enjoying his new-found power, he decided to go after the second group of youngsters he'd driven out of the church-yard. Although none of them had recognised him, he'd recognised them all right, because the day he'd been an advertising hoarding for the Fig Leaf wine bar, the same group of young-sters had followed him around Failsham for the best part of two hours, wolf-whistling and jeering at him. One of the girls had even tried to take a peep under his sandwich board. He was convinced it was one of them who'd stolen the board that day.

If they couldn't congregate in the churchyard, he reckoned they'd go to the next best place, the Market Square. There he found them, stood idly around, passing a bottle of cider back and forth between themselves.

The minute Johnny came into the square, he saw them look around frantically and start complaining about the noise. Realising they hadn't seen him, he decided to have a bit of fun. He stepped into an alleyway and hid from view.

"What is it? Where's it coming from?" he heard them say. "First the church – now here! What's going on? It's doing my head in!"

Johnny sniggered to himself on hearing this. One of the group suggested they go to the supermarket car park and the others agreed. Johnny stepped out of his hiding place to see the group move off. He knew a shortcut. He'd cut them off. He ran out of the square in the opposite direction to that taken by the youngsters. He took the road which ran diagonally to the Market Square, and at its end took a sharp left and sprinted along the road, at the end of which was the supermarket. It was closed for the night. Johnny jumped behind a row of recycling containers and waited for the group to appear. He heard them before he saw them, when they all began speaking at once:

"It's that noise again!" "Where's it coming from?" "It's following us!"

Johnny had to put his hand in his mouth to stop himself from laughing out loud when one of the girls said, "You don't think we've upset a ghost do you? I'm never going back to the graveyard again!"

Felix roared with laughter when Johnny rang him to tell him this. "That does it. I don't care what Mirabella and the Curate say. I'm definitely getting one fitted – I don't care if it alienates the young people or not!"

CHAPTER THIRTY-FOUR

That Old White Magick

I

Johnny, Jack and Charity turned up at Jane's back door just moments after Maria had called to say that she and Lena (the white witch) were on their way. The evening had been chosen by Lena herself due to the configuration of the moon and the stars. Jane glanced at the night sky as she showed her guests indoors, and saw there a Cheshire-Cat moon.

The evening wasn't a warm one, and her guests were all wrapped up snugly in thick fleeces, sheepskin snow boots, woollen hats and gloves. Jane poured Johnny and Charity a cup of warm mulled wine from the stove, and Jack a warm apple juice – drinks she thought befitted the occasion.

"If this doesn't work, there's someone on the internet who says he get can rid of mice by asking them to leave. He says he can talk the language of mice," Jack said.

"Bearing in mind how many mice there are in the world, that must be one of the world's most commonly spoken languages," Jane said.

Another knock on the door told her Maria and Lena had arrived. Maria, Jane couldn't help noticing, was looking rather jubilant. For reasons not yet explained, she was holding a folded up card table. She too was dressed warmly against the cold. Lena, on the other hand, wore only a long, skin-tight, sleeveless, low-cut, scarlet silk dress, as though she was stopping off to perform a spot of witchcraft, before going to a dinner dance. Maybe she was, Jane thought to herself. In some ways, Lena reminded Jane of Lucy Erpingham. Somewhat plump, it had to be said, yet with enough youthful self-confidence to feel no qualms about squeezing herself uncomfortably into clothes which emphasised every bulging inch.

Lena's long hair was the brightest red, and in keeping with the spectacle, she wore a great deal of jewellery: rings on each finger, numerous bracelets on each arm, a long three-chained earring in one ear, and a simple jet ball in the other. The large rucksack on her back somewhat spoiled the effect, but the forked willow stick in her hand more than made up for it.

Just as Jane was thinking, "Very witchy," Lena spoke.

With a sweep of her hair back across her shoulders, and the armful of silver bracelets jangling together noisily, she announced: "To the summerhouse!" She pointed the willow branch in its direction, and swept out of the kitchen towards it, followed by the others.

Lena placed her rucksack on the summerhouse's floor and knelt down. Just as Jane was wondering whether they were all meant to kneel before the rucksack and worship it, Lena removed from it a small copper bowl, a plastic box containing dried sage, and to the surprise of everyone in the room, a sugar mouse.

"An effigy of the creature is essential. The spirits need to know what they're to banish," she explained, dropping the sage into the bowl. This and the sugar mouse were placed in the centre of the floor, and the sage lit. "Now we must move outside and locate the best place for us to cast our spell," Lena said earnestly.

She got to her feet, put on her rucksack and went outside. Everyone followed her in single file. Maria, still holding the card table came last, leaving the door open. The sage was left to burn, its smoke suffusing the small room.

Lena held the forked willow stick horizontally in front of her with her right hand as she led the party across the garden. She stopped about halfway across, and holding the willow stick with both hands, moved it to the left and the right. Jane was surprised when it acted as a dowsing rod and appeared to jolt slightly. When it did, Lena said, "This is it! This will be our sacred space. Maria please put up the altar, while I make our magick circle."

Maria opened the trestle card table while Lena removed a salt cellar from her rucksack and used it to pour a white salt circle on the lawn, leaving Jane to pray that salt didn't irreparably damage grass.

"We are now ready. Because it is your house, Jane, you must stand there, just inside the circle, facing your home," Lena said, pointing to a spot immediately inside the salt circle, which put Jane staring at her house. "Jack, Johnny, Charity and Maria, you will form the four squares of the circle." No one asked how a circle could have four squares. Instead, they solemnly moved into position. Johnny stood a few feet away from Jane, at a slight angle to the house. Jack a few feet from him, Charity came next, her back to the house, and Maria stood next to her. "Now please all hold hands."

This they all did, even though it involved each of them stretching their arms out as far as they could. While Jane was beginning to wonder if this wasn't some practical joke on Maria's behalf, along the lines of the emperor's new clothes, Lena laid four plastic containers out on the card table altar. One of these she carried with her over to Johnny.

"You are North," she informed him, opening the box on which was written North. She removed some items from it, which she stood on the upturned empty box at Johnny's feet. Jane glanced at the objects. There was a brown candle, some cloves and an incense burner. Without warning, Lena walked over to one of Jane's flowerbeds and helped herself to a handful of soil. She also tugged at a tuft of moss from the lawn. She returned to lay these on the box by Johnny's feet. Out of the corner of her eye, Jane saw Lena light the candle and the incense burner, which she waved in the air. If Jane wasn't mistaken, she could smell Acacia.

"Beings of the earth, feeders of life," Lena said, "welcome to our sacred space. We ask you to banish from Jane's life the beings which have entered it. We ask you to banish them and stand firm and protect Jane and her home from more like them."

She made a circle in the air with the incense burner, and repeated it three times. She placed it onto the ground, next to the flickering candle then returned to the altar for her next box. This was marked West. She took it over to Jack and placed it at his feet. Inside it was an amber candle, a sea shell, coral and some nettles. Lena looked embarrassed. "I forgot to say you must bring with you a glass of water from the house."

"Okay," Jack said, in his usual good-natured way. As he ran towards the house, Lena called out to him, "Also bring parsley."

He glanced at Jane, who said, "There's a box in the cupboard next to the fridge, it's dried, which I hope is okay."

Jack disappeared into the kitchen, to appear moments later with a box of dried parsley in one hand and a glass of water in the other. Lena took both from him and placed the glass of water alongside the other objects on the box. As before, she lit both candle and the incense, then began her incantation.

"Beings of water, bringers of rains of life, welcome to our sacred space. We ask you to banish from Jane's life the beings which have entered it. We ask you to banish them and to stand firm and protect Jane and her home from more like them."

As before, she moved the incense burner around in a circle three times. It was now Charity's turn.

"You are South," Lena informed her.

This time a golden candle, some amber beads and the dried parsley were used. The candle was lit, so too some eucalyptus essence. This time the incantation was said to the bringers of fire. Jane glanced up at the sky. There wasn't a cloud in it – the bright crescent moon, and the stars – were all perfectly visible in the night sky. This Jane viewed as a good sign.

At Maria's feet Lena laid some aniseed seeds, some lava and a yellow candle. The spell this time was repeated to the bringers of the air, the bringers of the breath of life. Just as Jane had thought it was all over, Lena stood behind the altar. On it she placed a black candle and some fur. Jane assumed this was some of the mouse's fur, retrieved by Maria, but did not ask. Lena lit the candle. She dropped the fur into it. This immediately caught fire and burnt until it was all gone.

While Lena chanted to the elements of the earth, air, fire and water and asked them to hear her words, Jane allowed herself a quick glance across the field next door, to make sure there wasn't anyone filming the spectacle. She still wasn't convinced that this whole thing wasn't just a practical joke. Thankfully the field was empty.

"Help our friends leave the little house where they are trapped and return to the wild to their brothers and sisters, to their family and friends," Lena chanted. "So mote it be! Keep the creatures away from here now and forever more."

There was one more "So mote it be!" before Lena was bidding goodbye to the spirits. At Maria's feet she blew both candle and incense out. "Eastern spirit, thank you for your presence and your powers! Blow strongly! Hail and farewell!"

Eastern spirit duly addressed, she walked round to each of the party in reverse and repeated her spell for each of the elements, bidding them farewell in turn. "Burn brightly," she said to fire. "Flow powerfully," she said to water. "Nurture well," she instructed earth, finally telling the group, "the space is released. You can now let go of each other's hands."

It was over. Jane was pleased. She was rather cold and was looking forward to another glass of mulled wine.

"What happens now?" Johnny asked.

"What happens is that I'll warm up the mulled wine," Jane said, glad of an excuse to go inside. As she walked indoors, she hoped her cynicism didn't lesson the power of Lena's spells.

II

"Give it twenty-four hours," Lena explained once everybody was back in Jane's living room. Everyone apart from Jack (who had gone home to bed) held a cup of the warm mulled wine.

"If the mice are still here, you'll need to perform a daytime spell," she instructed. "You must return to the same spot, but this time at midday, where under the light of the midday sun, you must hold up a mirror to the sun and chant,

'Mice, be you away.

Banished by the light of day.

So mote it be!'

Say that three times, and I promise you they'll all go."

Jane wasn't quite sure she would be prepared to do this. In fact she was quite certain she wouldn't. If the mice weren't gone by tomorrow, she wouldn't be standing in her garden casting spells by sunbeam, she'd be in a hardware shop buying a few traps and some poison. Nonetheless, she nodded at Lena's words and repeated the spell.

"Mice be you away

Banished by the light of day.

So Mote it be!"

As she spoke these words, something that had been niggling her since Lena had cast her spell in the garden, came to the forefront of her mind and she realised what it was.

"Lena, if I were to list a collection of objects, apparently random, but which were found together, would you be able to tell me whether or not they could have been used for black magick?"

The objects Jane was referring to were those found by Felix in the graveyard. She listed them: "A twenty pound note, torn in half; a china Ganesa, the Hindu goddess of prosperity, with her elephant head broken off; an empty bubble-making bottle, and a yellow caper candle."

"Did the candle have scratch marks?" Lena asked.

Jane thought back. She pictured it lying in the box held by Felix, and saw on it arrows pointing downwards. She'd noticed them at the time, but thought the scratcher bored, not malevolent. She said so.

"Classic black magick."

"Crikey!" Charity said.

"Even the bubble bottle?" Jane asked.

Lena nodded. "Any halfway competent witch can incant a spell and put it inside a bubble, be it good or bad, and send it off in the direction of the person for whom it's intended. Please list the items for me again."

Jane repeated them. Lena thought awhile, then pronounced, "Our witch is trying to bring financial ruin to someone."

"Crikey!" Charity repeated.

"You think someone is practising black magick in the churchyard, Jane?" Johnny said.

"Not just in the churchyard, and not just financial ruin either," she replied. "I also think I know who the culprit may be."

She recalled the words she'd overheard at the bikers' rally – "It's the old green-eyed monster, mate. It makes people go stir crazy, look what happened to old Kenny!" –then thought back to the upside-down horseshoe she'd come across at the roadside the day she'd released the mouse, and the tiny play-dough models she'd stood on. She'd thought them the work of local children, and maybe they were, but now she thought about it, the play-dough she'd peeled from her sole looked as though it was moulded into the shape of a woman, and there'd been a stick, causing her to wonder if what she actually stood on had been the model of a solitary woman, with a stick through her heart, lying next to a man and woman, holding hands. Three stick people deliberately left by the side of the route taken every day by a happy young couple, by someone not so happy.

"Who?" Maria asked.

Everyone in the room leaned forward.

"Hayley Payne."

Jane told the others in the room of her earlier encounter with Hayley, and the animosity expressed towards her cousin, Jess.

"Jess Payne? The girl whose wine bar I helped advertise?" Johnny said, "The Fig Leaf?"

"One and the same," Jane said.

"Hayley asked me for all the flyers I was giving out – I just thought she was greedy and pushing her luck 'cause of being Jess's cousin."

"Hayley's been jealous of Jess since they were children. I found the play-dough just down the lane from where you were the day Jess stopped and offered you work. Jess and Adam live just down that lane. I suspect they and the upside-down horse-shoe were intended to bring bad fortune to the relationship, and the items found in the churchyard, to the business. She may even have stolen the Fig Leaf's sandwich board, for whatever purpose."

"We passed Hayley on the way to Dabney Farm standing in a field waving her arms about and spinning around and around, until she fell over. We just thought she'd eaten one too many magic mushrooms," Johnny said.

"Probably had," both Maria and Charity said simultaneously.

"She was casting a spell," Lena said.

"The guy what owns the farm said she'd asked him for one of his chickens – he thought she'd wanted to set them free, but maybe she wanted to use its blood in some potion?" Johnny suggested.

"When I wouldn't help her try and ruin her cousin's happiness, she must have decided to go down another route," Jane said. "I don't think the liquid Felix found bubbling in the churchyard was left by any junkie, I think it was some witch's brew concocted by young Hayley to bring some ill to her cousin. Felix's son didn't hear a name spoken that evening, what he heard was the end of Hayley saying, 'So Mote It Be!'"

"Crikey!" Charity said again. "The things people get up to. Wait a minute? Didn't you say Jess gave you a slice of an apple pie Hayley had baked her as a warming present? Can evil be baked in a pie?" she asked Lena.

Everyone, apart from Jane, looked horrified. Lena put her hand over her mouth and said, rather melodramatically Jane thought, "It can. Kitchen black witchery is one of the most dangerous kinds."

Johnny jumped to his feet and clutched his stomach. Charity ran to one side and grabbed his arm and Maria the other. "What's going to happen?" Maria asked.

"Will it be quick?" Charity said.

"Am I going to have bad luck for the rest of my life?" Johnny wanted to know.

Unseen by the others, all of whom were focused on Johnny, Jane rolled her eyes.

"The dark powers contained in that food will not harm you. You are dealing with a professional," Lena said. "One whose black magic is targeted."

"I think our dark witch is less professional sorceress, more inadequate young woman getting spells out of a library book. Nothing more sinister," Jane said.

"It's even worse when amateurs get involved," Lena said, despairingly. "They don't understand what they're doing. They start conjuring up the spirits of evil. They bring bad karma on themselves." Lena started to chant:

'An ye harm none, do what ye will.

What ye send forth comes back to Thee,

So ever mind the Rule of Three!'

"I must stop her, before it's too late. There's nothing more poisonous than bad karma!" Lena said. "Do you know where I might find her?"

Whilst Jane still thought Hayley more silly than dangerous, she knew what it was like to have an annoying pest in one's life, and for Jess and Adam's sake wanted to put a stop to it. "As a matter of fact I do, and it's somewhere I need to visit anyway."

III

Johnny returned a few minutes after Jane had shown everyone out.

"In all the excitement, I forgot to give you this," he said, handing her the Mosquito, although Jane wasn't sure why. "If the mouse is resistant to white magick, this'll do the trick," he explained. "Animals have very sensitive hearing – like kids. I tried it out on Jack on the way over here: 'Make it stop! Make it stop!'" he said, mimicking Jack. "If it's still there, this thing shrieking all day and all night will get rid of it. You can leave it in the summerhouse all year, if needs be – we can't hear it."

"Won't Jack have to move?" she said, taking it nonetheless.

She placed the ringing Mosquito on the bookshelf of her summerhouse and left its door open.

CHAPTER THIRTY-FIVE

Saffron and Silk

Jane knew where Hayley could be found because she'd seen her a few days earlier working on a stall on Failsham market. Jane hadn't been surprised to see her there. Jane knew the stall's owner, Annette Gray, very well. As she'd explained to the others,

"Annette's most likely given Hayley a job despite others warning her not to, because that's her nature."

Jane arranged to meet Lena at the stall. They arrived a few minutes apart as agreed. Annette greeted Jane with a warm smile, which was reciprocated. Jane noticed Hayley slouching against the far end of the stall with a foot pressed against its wall, making not the slightest attempt to be civil to customers, let alone ask if they required service.

"Hayley, serve the other the lady, will you?" Annette said, motioning towards Lena.

"Oh, it's all right, I haven't decided what I want yet," Lena said, turning to study Hayley intently.

"How can I help you, Jane?" Annette asked.

"I want to bake my sister-in-law a simnel cake for Easter, but I'm out of saffron," she explained.

A packet of saffron strands was placed in front of her.

"And some almond essence, if you have some."

This too was produced from the shelf behind the stall and handed to Jane, who paid for them.

Although she knew something was going to happen, even Jane was surprised when Lena suddenly placed one hand on her forehead and stretched the other out in front of her, pointing directly at Hayley. Lena started moving from side to side, as though having some sort of seizure. "You!" Lena said, moving her outstretched arm around in a circle. "You've been casting bad spells!"

Hayley turned white. She opened and shut her mouth.

"You've been casting dark spells to make bad things happen."

"No I haven't," Hayley protested.

"Do not lie to me. I am a white witch and I can always sense when someone is dabbling in the dark arts. You're a bad person and a disgrace to the profession of witches."

"I... I..." the girl said, unable to continue.

"You must stop. Now!" Lena commanded. "The Wiccan creed can not allow such behaviour to continue unchecked. You are awakening powers you can't begin to understand."

"If I could interrupt this," Annette said. Everyone turned to look at her, apart from Hayley who looked as though she was in a trance, unable to move. "I would appreciate it if you two would continue your barney away from my stall."

"I have said all that needs to be said," Lena said, sweeping her shawl over one shoulder and her long hair over the other. She turned to leave the stall, but took only a couple of steps before pausing to dramatically spin around and point at

Hayley, "If you dabble in the dark arts again, I will seek you out…" Lena threatened.

"I won't, I won't, I promise!" Hayley said, sounding as though she was absolutely terrified.

With these words Lena walked away leaving Hayley looking as though she couldn't decide whether to run after Lena and beg forgiveness from Wicca, or flee to Kathmandu.

"Get your stuff and get out," Annette told her.

Hayley didn't need to be told twice. Bag and coat in hand she ran from the stall, visibly shaking.

"What on earth was that about?" Annette asked.

"I believe one was a white witch, and the other dark witch," Jane said, by way of explanation.

"People warned me about her, but she seemed so nice when I interviewed her. But then you never can tell, can you?" Annette said. "Can I interest you in a nice piece of silk ribbon to tie around your cake, Jane?"

"You know, I think you can."

CHAPTER THIRTY-SIX

Mr Jonathan

Ever since she'd married, Jane had baked a simnel cake for Easter. Even though Hugh was no longer with her, she didn't intend this Easter to be any different. Jane's mother had been a keen baker, as had her grandmother, and the simnel cake recipe she followed was her grandmother's recipe.

It didn't matter how many times Jane had baked the cake, she always liked to be able to refer to the recipe, if needs be. It was written on a separate sheet of paper in her grandmother's hands. The page on which it was written, had, over the decades, become stained, and the paper ripped and repeatedly resealed by tape. Eventually Jane had taken the recipe to be laminated – making it easy to prop up against the kitchen wall – which was where it was now.

She was in the process of rolling tiny marzipan balls in the palms of her hands with which to decorate the top of the cake, when Charity arrived on her doorstep.

"I came to see if the mouse had left," she said.

Jane knew full well that with Johnny called out on an emergency over an overhanging branch, and Jack spending the afternoon with Polly, Charity was at a loose end.

"I'll put the kettle on," Jane said. "The mouse has gone. I checked this morning. Not a trace. Not a dropping."

"So witchcraft really works, eh?"

"Either that or the Mosquito. I couldn't possibly say which."

"Very funny," Charity said of Jane's inadvertent wordplay. "I always thought witchcraft involved dancing naked under a waning moon, banging a tambourine and imbibing restricted substances. That was all a bit tame."

"You sound almost disappointed," Jane said laughing. "I don't know what to make of it all, but I'm thinking of getting Lena back again when the greenfly arrive. You know how much I hate chemicals."

The conversation turned to Johnny's father. Charity was indignant. "He never gave his own son a second thought. What kind of man is he? Can you imagine how Johnny felt when he learnt that?"

"I'm not trying to defend him in any way, but remember the man who left was a young and thoughtless one. The man I met was a dying, reflective one who asked for his son's forgiveness. If you remember, we were worried what we'd do if his father wasn't interested in having anything to do with him. At least that didn't happen. His father may have extended the olive branch far too late, at the least he extended it."

"I suppose so. How do you explain the letter to Stella? Do you think the lady who sent Sue the postcard from Blackpool, wrote it?"

"I don't think so. She'd have no reason to send it. I think it was Sue. I rather suspect what Stella received was a note Pete once sent Sue, probably when they were still courting, and years later she forged his writing on the envelope and sent the note to Stella."

"Why?"

"To see if she knew where he was. I suspect she followed Stella on the day in question, to see if she went or not, and if she did, whether she met up with him."

"That's quite sad."

"More than quite."

"All this has made Johnny start asking when we're going to get married and have our own family."

"Charity, that's wonderful news," Jane said, giving her neighbour a hug. "If you take his name, you'll be Charity Lambert. That's a nice name. I've always quite liked being Jane Hetherington, but Hugh's poor mother became Hettie Hetherington when she married, but one just can't anticipate these things when one names a child. My Adele is now Adele Smithson. Not bad."

"Hold on, let's not get carried away," Charity replied hurriedly. "He hasn't got down on bended knee or anything yet, he just wants me to think about it. I don't know if I even want to."

"I thought that's what you wanted?"

Here, Charity became unusually coy.

"I did, but you've got to be careful about getting what you wish for, haven't you?"

Jane wasn't sure she agreed with what Charity had just said. She and Hugh had known each other for eight months when they'd become engaged. It was exactly what she wished for at the time, and she'd never regretted it. She knew what the problem was, right enough. Charity still didn't trust Johnny not to disappear again. This was something Jane couldn't help with, she'd have to resolve this one herself.

"At this rate you and Johnny will be celebrating your Ruby Wedding Anniversary without ever having made it up the aisle," she teased.

She returned to her cake, where she made another tiny marzipan ball in her hands. She placed the tiny ball on the cake. "Where's Jack taking Polly?" she asked, thinking it better she change the subject.

"For coffee in Southstoft. This is their second date. I'll be buying a hat soon," she wailed.

"Sooner than I'll be buying one for your wedding," Jane joked.

"What are you doing for Easter Sunday, Jane? We're spending it at home. You're welcome to join us. We're having turkey."

"That's kind, but I'm driving up to my sister-in-law's tomorrow morning. It's given me a nice excuse to bake. Old Charlie Moon's being buried next week. I'll drive from their place to the funeral – it's closer than from here."

"Charlie Moon's passed away?"

"A couple of days ago. His grandson Dean rang – he thought I might like to pay my last respects, which I would."

At that moment, Johnny appeared at the back door. His first words were, "I've got us a goose..."

"A goose!" Charity squealed. "Why did you get us a goose? I've just taken the turkey out of the freezer. We'll have to freeze it. The turkey's already defrosting."

"We definitely can't do that, my dear" Johnny said. "It would be inhumane."

"What on earth does that mean?" Charity demanded. She slapped her hand on her forehead. "Johnny, don't tell me the goose is still alive?"

"Okay, I won't tell you."

"I'm not wringing its throat!"

"I should hope not."

"Where is it?"

"In the kitchen."

"The kitchen? What about Addison? Geese are vicious creatures."

"Addison? Cripes I forgot about him!" Johnny said, literally rushing through the door, followed quickly by Charity, and much more sedately by Jane.

When Jane reached her neighbour's house she found the back door wide open and Charity and Johnny in the kitchen, staring into a shoe box held by Johnny.

"He's okay," he said.

"Who's okay?" Jane asked, "Oh! Good heavens!" she said, looking into the shoe box, where a tiny gosling nestled next to its broken shell, cheeping furiously.

"He's just hatched," Charity felt the need to explain, tears welling up in her eyes.

"Where did you find him, Johnny?" Jane asked.

"You know I had to rush off to Giles Marham's place to cut down that dangerous branch over the public footpath?" Johnny said. "Well, afterwards we went round to his place to see some abandoned goose eggs that him and his missus were hatching in the Aga. When we got there this little fellow's egg was jumping up and down. None of the others showed any signs of life – they were all stone cold – except this little guy. The

Marham's didn't know what to do – they're going on holiday tomorrow – so I said I'd take him. Couldn't see him left to die could I? Not the sole survivor."

"Well, no, not really," Jane said.

"I'm going to look after him until he's old enough to release back into the wild," Johnny said.

"I'm not sure you can do that with birds, Johnny," Charity said. "Don't they imprint or something? Jane?"

"Don't ask me. I know next to nothing about geese, although if I'm going to have one as a near neighbour, I guess I'll have to learn more about them," she said.

"We'll have to keep him away from Addison till he's old enough to stand up for himself, then we'll have to keep Addison away from him," Charity said, apparently having decided to keep him as a pet. She stared down on the little hatchling. "Hello newly hatched one. Would you like some wild bird seed?"

"Jack wants us to call it Mr Jonathan Goose if it's a boy, and Polly if it's a girl," Johnny told her.

"Sweet," Charity replied, still clucking at the tiny goose, leaving Jane unsure whether her comments referred to Jack's suggested names or the hatchling.

CHAPTER THIRTY-SEVEN

Month's End

On her way back home, Jane's new Smartphone peeped to tell her she had a new e-mail. Once indoors, she opened and read it. It was from Lucy Erpingham's sister, Jodie Narbade.

'Lucy confessed immediately – didn't have much choice with that recording you sent us. She thought we were the ones who'd claimed to be the real winners.

Her version of events is that when she found the blue envelope in the crisps, she expected to win a tenner and thought it was a joke when she read the words:-

Congratulations you've just won £100,000! Yes! £100,000!

She said she ran out the door with the prize, then went back to grab the receipt. I'd bought the crisps and wine on the way back from work, and the receipt was still lying on the table. Her excuse for not saying anything is that she wanted to check it was genuine before telling us, but when the company said she really had found the winning envelope, she asked for the money to be paid into her bank account because she just couldn't resist it. She went for the no-publicity option – obviously. When the money arrived she kept staring at her bank statement. All she could see was the noughts. It was more money than she'd ever had or was likely to have in her life. She could clear her debts and still have masses left over. Enough to buy anything she wanted. That's what she said. Then she started spending and she couldn't stop. She bought everyone she knew, everything they wanted. She paid for everything. Everyone wanted to be her friend. She didn't know what to say about where she got all that money, so she avoided us. She thought if she gave up work it would be too suspicious, also she knew the money wouldn't last forever. She said every time she thought about us, she felt guilty. I should **** think so!

She admits she went crazy. There's hardly any money left, you know. She's spent nearly all of it. The little***! When I think of what we could have done with it! She's given us what's left, but that's not much, not compared to how much there was. We'll never see the rest. She says she'll repay us, but that's all pie in the sky. My husband still can't bear to be in the same room as her. I had to talk him out of going to the police. He wants to sue her, but like I said, what's the point? She's spent the money. Besides, she's still my kid sister and I love her despite everything she's done.

The only consolation is that she's back in our lives. Mum and dad can't believe what she's done either, but at least she's not avoiding them in the street any more. I asked her if it was worth it, and she said it wasn't: "I missed you so much, Jode, and mum and dad. Not being able to talk to you was hateful. It was like part of my life wasn't there." She even said it was a relief everything was out in the open, and we can try getting back to being a normal family, although I think that will take some time.'

252

The e-mail ended with Lucy's sister thanking Jane for all her help and asking her to e-mail over her invoice.

Jane replied: 'From my observation of your little sister, I do genuinely believe her remorse is heartfelt, and she is contrite for her actions. I wish you and your family all the best.

Jane Hetherington.'

When a case was over, Jane always liked to make a summary of its nature and outcome for her records and place a tick under the 'Case Solved' column, if at all possible. In this case it was, and with a tick in the box completed, Jane considered the case closed.

She sat back in her seat. All in all, she'd had a good month. She'd solved all her cases, saved a young couple from the Dark Eye, and finally rid herself of her rodent lodger. More importantly, she'd helped to bring some closure to Johnny's life, which would hopefully allow him to move on with the rest of it. All in all, she'd had a good month.

Now there was just Charlie Moon's funeral left.

CHAPTER THIRTY-EIGHT

Shine On Charlie Moon!

Charlie Moon's funeral was held at a crematorium close to Greenfields. Charlie's whole family were in attendance, including its latest addition – six-month-old Daisy – Charlie Moon's great-granddaughter. Also present were some of the residents from Greenfields, including Ted and Betsy Cully, and Bea Applegate. Dean and his mother met the mourners at the door.

"Thank you for coming, Mrs Hetherington," Dean said to Jane when she arrived. "Mum, this is the lady who went to Greenfields for us, to check up on Granddad."

While Dean's mother greeted other mourners, Dean took Jane to one side. With a quick glance to make sure no one else was listening, he whispered, "They found him dead in someone else's bed, you know?"

"Really! I thought that only happened to Nelson Rockefeller?"

"She was a sixty-six-year old widow. He'd told her he was only sixty-nine!" Dean said with a laugh. "She couldn't believe it when we told her how old he really was. Randy old bugger."

When Jane finally took her seat for Charlie's funeral, she could honestly say she was glad she'd met him, but was even gladder she hadn't known him any better than she had.

CHAPTER THIRTY-NINE

An Ode to an Unwanted Lodger:
AKA The Artful Dodger

There once was a field mouse called Aleckski, who thought the outdoors rather dicey.

Nature was far too red in tooth and claw, for our friendly little herbivore.

Not wishing his to be a death foretold, he scurried in from the cold.

When asked to leave, he got peeved, demanding instead lots of cheese!

Mousetraps they came, and mousetraps they went, but Aleckski he was adamant.

The grass on the other side wasn't greener – it was just a whole lot meaner.

He could not be persuaded to change his mind, oh no, not our miniature mastermind.

Quarry and hunter were at daggers drawn, with one about to reach for the Warfarin.

When suddenly there was an answer, why not call in a spirit-omancer?

To the spirits our witch made a plea – please remove the mouse humanely.

The effect could not than less astound – our friend became disinclined to hang around.

And so our tale did not end tragically, in fact it finished rather magically.

And so concluded our game of cat and mouse, and the unlawful occupation of a summerhouse!

A new poem by Stanman.

Coming soon from Nina Jon:-

Jane Hetherington's Adventures in Detection: 4

April

Made in the USA
Charleston, SC
27 March 2012